THE RED SIGNAL

Grace Livingston Hill

THE RED SIGNAL

G.K. Hall & Co. • **Chivers Press**
Thorndike, Maine USA   **Bath, England**

This Large Print edition is published by G.K. Hall & Co., USA
and by Chivers Press, England.

Published in 1999 in the U.S. by arrangement with
Munce Publishing.

Published in 1999 in the U.K. by arrangement with
Munce Publishing Company.

U.S. Softcover 0-7838-0420-2   (Paperback Series Edition)
U.K. Harcover   0-7540-3615-4   (Chivers Large Print)
U.K. Softcover 0-7540-3616-2   (Camden Large Print)

The text of this Large Print edition is unabridged.
Other aspects of the book may vary from the original edition.

Set in 16 pt. Plantin by Al Chase.

Printed in the United States on permanent paper.

British Library Cataloguing in Publication Data available

Library of Congress Cataloging in Publication Data

Hill, Grace Livingston, 1865–1947.
    The red signal / Grace Livingston Hill.
      p.   cm.
    ISBN 0-7838-0420-2 (lg. print : sc : alk. paper)
    1. Large type books. I. Title.
    [PS3515.I486R44 1999]
    813′.52—dc21   98-44165

THE RED SIGNAL

1

Hilda Lessing stood hesitating fearfully before the wide expanse of railroad tracks that seemed to be fairly bristling with menacing engines, some moving, some standing still. In her bewilderment she could not be sure which were moving and which were standing still. They all seemed alive, waiting to pounce upon her if she stirred.

The conductor had told her, when he put her off the express, that the other train made good connections, and she had no time to waste. He had pointed across all those tracks, and across them she must go. She made a wild dash, accomplished half the distance, and suddenly found herself snatched from the very teeth of a flying express that had appeared like a comet out of the mêlée, and held in strong arms against a bit of rail fence that traversed the space between the tracks for a little distance.

It seemed ages that she clung with trembling arms to a big rough shoulder, her body pressed against the fence, one hand still gripping the suitcase jammed between her and the fence, while an interminable train rushed, car after car, past her reeling brain, the hot breath of its going blasting her cheeks. To add to the horror, another train dashed into sight on the other side of the frail fence and tore along in the opposite direction. She felt like a leaf in a crevice with a great roaring avalanche on either side. If she should let go her feeble hold of the rescuer for a single instant, or if he failed her, she was lost. Her horrified eyes were strained and fascinated with the fearful spectacle till it seemed she could bear it no longer; then she closed them with a shiver and dropped her face to the broad blue jean shoulder that offered the only relief.

The strong arms seemed to hold her closer with a reassuring pressure that comforted her. The rushing of the train was growing less as if some spell had it within control now, and she felt herself lifted and borne swiftly beyond the noise and confusion. She dared not open her eyes until he put her down upon a quiet bench at the far end of the platform away from the crowds.

She dimly felt that people were looking curiously, excitedly, after her, and that the trainmen, with startled faces, were calling out something to her companion; but she paid no heed to any of them. She only saw his face bending solicitously over her, his pleasant eyes so brown and merry, and heard his cheery voice:

"Say, kid, that was a close call! Didn't you know any better than to cross those tracks with both fliers due? Where was the station man, I'd like to know, that he let you start?"

"Oh!" gasped Hilda, turning whiter than ever. "I didn't know! I couldn't find a way across, and I had to make my train!" Then the tears came in a flood of nervous reaction and she dropped her face into her hands and sobbed.

The man in the blue overalls sidled up to her in dismay and put his big arm awkwardly around her, forgetful of his amused comrades not far away.

"There! There! Kid! Don't cry! It's all over, and you're perfectly safe!"

He patted her slender shaking shoulders gently with a big blackened hand, and looked helplessly down at the girl.

"What train were you meaning to take?" he asked with sudden inspiration.

Hilda lifted a pair of drenched blue eyes, large and wide, with a new fear, and started to her feet.

"Oh! The train to Platt's Crossing! Has it gone? I ought to hurry! Which way do I go?"

The young man looked at his watch. He had nice hair and a handsome head. She liked the way the dark curl fell over his white forehead, and the strength of the bronzed neck above the jumper.

"You've plenty of time. Number ten isn't due for fifteen minutes. Come over to the restaurant and have a cup of coffee. That'll put some pep into you."

He seized the suitcase and led the way. She noticed that he did everything as if he were a gentleman. She liked the way he pulled out the chair and seated her at the table. He gave an order for sandwiches, coffee, baked apples and cream. It looked good to her after a night and morning of fasting.

"Do you live at Platt's Crossing?" His brown eyes were fixed pleasantly, respectfully upon her.

"No! That is — I live in Chicago — or I did till Father died. I'm going to work at Platt's Crossing."

She spoke as if it were an unpleasant fact that had not yet become familiar enough to lose the pain of its expression.

"You look young to go to work," he said kindly, interestedly. "What line? Telephone girl or stenography?"

The color stole up under her clear skin.

"Neither," she said bravely. "It's a truck farm. They're Germans my uncle knows. I'm to help. Housework, I suppose. I'm going to try to like it, but I wanted to teach. I had finished high school and was going to Normal next fall if Father hadn't died. But something happened to our money and I had to take this place. Mother's got a place as matron in an orphan asylum, where she could take my little brother with her. It isn't very pleasant, but it was the best that we could do."

"That's tough luck, kid!" said the young man sympathetically, "but brace up! If you've got it in you to teach you'll get your chance yet. Are you German?"

"No," said the girl decidedly. "Father was. He was born in Germany. He liked this country, though, and didn't keep running back to Germany every year the way my uncle does. But Mother and I are Americans. Mother was born in Chicago."

"Well, you'd better keep your eyes open, kid! Those German truck farms have been getting a bad name since the war broke out. There are lots of spies around just now. You can't tell what you may come across."

There was a twinkle of fun in his eyes, but a strain of earnestness in his voice. The girl looked at him in wide-eyed wonder.

"You don't suppose there would be any such thing as that?" she asked, dropping her spoon. "I thought spies were just newspaper talk. Our high school teacher used to say so."

"Well, there are plenty of spies around all right!" he said seriously. "It's not all newspaper talk. But don't you worry. It isn't likely they'll come around you, and you might not know them for spies if they did."

"Oh! I should be so frightened!" she said, her hand fluttering to her throat. "What do people do when they discover spies?"

"Just lie low and send word to Washington as quick as they can. But don't look like that, kid; I was just talking nonsense!"

She tried to answer his smile with another.

"I know I'm silly," she said contritely, "but it

seems so dreadful to come to this strange place among people I don't know anything about."

"Oh, you'll come out all right. It won't be so bad as you think. They'll likely turn out to be fine."

She took a deep breath and smiled bravely.

"I don't know what Mother would say if she knew I was talking to you," she remarked anxiously. "She brought me up never to speak to strange young men. But you've been so kind saving my life! Only I wouldn't like to have you think I'm that kind of a girl —"

"Of course not!" he said indignantly. "Anybody could see that with a glance. I hope you haven't thought I was fresh, either. I saw you were all in and needed a little jollying up. I guess those two expresses sort of introduced us, didn't they? I'm Dan Stevens. My father is — has a position — that is, he *works* on the railroad, and I'm engineer just at present on number five freight. I'll be glad to be of service to you at any time."

"My name is Hilda Lessing," said the girl shyly. "You certainly have been kind to me. I shan't ever forget that I would have been killed if it hadn't been for you. I guess you might have been killed. too. You were very brave, jumping in between those trains after me. I shan't feel quite so lonesome and homesick now, knowing there's someone I know between Platt's Crossing and Chicago."

"Oh, that wasn't anything!" said the young

man lightly. "That's part of the railroad business, you know. But say! It's rank to be homesick! Suppose I give you a signal as I pass Platt's Crossing. I get there at 2:05 usually, unless we're late. It will maybe cheer you up to let you know there's somebody around you know. I'll give three long blasts and two short ones. That'll be to say: 'Hello! How are you? Here's a friend!' I know where that truck farm is, right along the railroad before you get to the bridge, about a quarter of a mile this side. There isn't much else at Platt's Crossing but that farm. We stop to take on freight sometimes. Here, I'll tell you what you do. If everything's all right and you think things are going to go you just hang a towel or apron or something white out your window, or on the fence rail somewhere. I'll be watching for it. That will be like saying: 'I'm very well, thank you.' Won't that make you feel a little more at home?"

"It certainly will. It will be something to look forward to," said Hilda smiling shyly. "I shan't be half as much afraid if I know there is somebody going by to whom I could signal if I got into trouble. Of course, I know I won't, but you understand."

"Of course," said the engineer rising. "That's all right. If you get into trouble or find that spy or anything, you can hang out a red rag for a danger signal, and then I'll know there is something that needs to be looked after. See? Now, I guess we had better beat it. It's time for that train of yours. I'm glad to have met you. You're a mighty plucky little girl and I honor you."

He pushed back his chair and picked up the suitcase. She noticed again the ease of every movement, as if he were waiting on the greatest lady in the land. Then the train boomed in; he put her on, found a seat for her, touched his greasy cap with courteous grace and was gone. A moment more and she was started on her way to Platt's Crossing.

She paid little heed to the landscape by the way, for she was going over and over again all that had happened since she set her first timid step across the labyrinth of tracks, and was caught from sudden death by the strong arms of the young engineer. Various sensations that had hardly seemed to register at the time now came back to make her heart leap and her pulses thrill with horror or wonder or a strange new pleasure. How strong he had been! How well he had protected her, with never a quiver of his sturdy frame while those monster trains leaped by! How little and safe and cared-for she had felt in spite of her fear! And how thoughtful he had been, taking her to get some lunch and planning to cheer her up a little on her first lonely day at the new home! Perhaps Mother would not quite think that was proper, for she had warned her many times to have nothing to do with strange young men, but, then, Mother surely would understand if she could see him. He was a perfect gentleman, even if he did wear blue jean overalls; and besides, they would never likely see each other again. What possible harm could a whistle and a white towel hanging out a window do? He wouldn't likely do it but once, and, of course, she wouldn't; and it was pleasant to feel that there was someone to whom she could appeal if anything really frightened her, which, of course, there wouldn't. And, anyhow, he had saved her life and she must be polite to him.

It seemed ages since she had left her mother and little brother the day before to start on this long journey into the world. She seemed to have come a lifetime in experience since then. What would it be like at the farm? Was she going to like it, or was it going to be the awful stretch of emptiness that she had pictured it ever since Uncle Otto had told her she was to go? Somehow, since she had talked with the young engineer there was just the least bit of a rift in the darkness of her despair. He had said that if she had it in her to teach she would get her opportunity. Well, she could be patient and wait. Meantime, it was pleasant to think of that handsome young man and the courteous way in which he had treated her. He reminded her of a picture she had once seen of a prince. True, he was not dressed in princely robes, but she was American enough to recognize a prince in spite of his attire.

She still had the dream of him in her mind

when she got out at Platt's Crossing and looked around bewildered at the loneliness of the landscape.

There was nothing more than a shanty for a station, and the only other building in sight was a dingy wooden house across some rough, plowed fields, with a large barn at a little distance from it.

She looked about in dismay for something else to guide her, and perceived a man coming toward her. He was attired in brown jeans with an old straw hat on his head, and he was as far as possible from any likeness to the young man who had put her on the train. Idealism soaring high and sweet above her head suddenly collapsed at her feet and she went forward to meet the stolid-looking man.

There was no kindly greeting, no lightning of the face, nor twinkling of the little pig eyes. She might have been a plow or a bag of fertilizer just deposited, for all the personality he allowed to her. He asked her if she was the girl from Chicago in much the same way he would have looked at the markings on some freight to be sure it was his before he went to the trouble of carrying it home.

Hilda had a shrinking notion that he was rather disappointed in her appearance. He pointed across the plowed ground to the forlorn house in the distance and told her she could go on up, they were waiting for her; as if it were her fault that she had not been there before.

Hilda picked up her heavy suitcase, looked dubiously at the long, rough road before her and glanced at the man. He had apparently forgotten her existence. He made no effort to carry her burden for her. With a sudden set of her firm little chin and a keen remembrance of the strong young engineer who had carried it so gallantly a little while before, she started bravely on her way, slowly, painfully toiling over the rough ground, and in her inexperience taking the hardest, longest way across the furrows.

The stolid woman who met her at the door with arms akimbo, furiously red face and small blue eyes that observed her appraisingly, was a fit mate for the man who had directed her to the house. She gave no smile of welcome. Her lips were thin and set, though she was not unkindly. Hilda gathered that her coming had not been exactly looked forward to with pleasure, and that her presence was regarded more in the light of an unpleasant necessity than that of a companionable helper, as her uncle would have had her think.

"So! You've come!" said the woman in a colorless voice.

"Yes!" said Hilda. "Is this Mrs. Schwarz?"

The woman nodded, meantime giving her closer scrutiny.

"You ain't so strong!" she announced sternly, as if the girl were somehow defrauding her of what she had a right to expect.

Hilda put down her suitcase and straightened her slender back, tilting her delicate chin just a shade.

"I'm never sick," she said coldly. She looked regretfully back across the rough way she had come to the friendly railroad tracks gleaming in the distance and wished she dared turn and flee. Then she saw the stolid man moving heavily across the field, and turned back to her fate.

"You can take it up to your room," the colorless voice directed, pointing to the suitcase. "Up the stairs und the first door in front. Ged in your vork cloes und cum down und help me. I haf mooch to do!"

Hilda fled up the stairs. A sudden desire to cry had stung in her eyes and crowded into her throat. She must not break down now, just at this first hour in her new home and before her employers.

She drew the door shut and noticed with joy that there was a lock. She turned the key softly and went to the one little window, looking out stealthily. Yes, it was on the side of the house toward the railroad track, whether front or back she could not tell, the house was of so nondescript a fashion. But her heart rejoiced that at least she would not have to maneuver and contrive to fling out her signal.

Opening her suitcase she took out a little white apron and hung it out the window by its strings.

18

She removed her hat. bathed her face, smoothed her hair, and changed her dress for a neat school gingham. She was about to go downstairs when a low distant rumble broke on her ear.

Hurrying to the window, she knelt on the floor and looked out. Yes, it was a freight train winding far down the valley, coming up the shining steel track. Was it his train? Would he remember to look or would he not expect her to have the signal ready before tomorrow?

Forgetful of her waiting mistress and the new duties below stairs, she knelt and watched the train crawl like a black writhing serpent up the track; and just as it drew near and was almost in front of her window the voice of her mistress sounded raucously up the passageway with insistency:

"I haf told you to hurry! You should cum down at vonce!" The tinge of German accent was stronger under excitement.

"Yes, in just a minute, Mrs. Schwarz!" called Hilda, turning her head excitedly from the window to answer. At that instant the clear piercing shriek of the whistle sounded forth:

——— ! ——— ! ——— ! —— ! —— !

The voice of the mistress was drowned beyond all hearing. Hilda leaned out of her window, caught the little white apron and fluttered it forth at arm's length. The train was opposite the house now, and the girl could distinctly see a cap waved from the caboose of the engine, although the distance across the fields was not short. Something happy leaped up in her heart, making her cheeks glow and her eyes shine. And then came the blast of the whistle again:

———— ! ———— ! ———— ! ——— ! ——— !

The train passed on over the big bridge, whose high stone arches reflected in the stream below; and echoing back its signal as it passed it wound on between the hills and was gone. Then Hilda got to her feet with illumined face and went down to meet her future. She had not even seen the young lout in cowhide boots and brown overalls who had appeared out of the clods of the earth it would seem, in color like unto them, and stood leaning against a fence, leering up at the window.

2

It seemed a lifetime to Hilda before they finally sat down to supper, although in reality it was but five o'clock. The mistress had spoken well when she had said there was much to be done. The girl, already weary with her journey and the excitement, was in no fit condition to plunge into the vortex of new duties which met her like a foe she had to face. Her back ached and her head throbbed as she bent her slender shoulders under the weight of big buckets of water and armfuls of wood which she was required to carry. Fresh from the classroom, having led a sheltered, guarded life hitherto, she staggered under duties that might have seemed easy to one accustomed to them. She grew white around the mouth and black under the eyes as she toiled on uncomplainingly, but she would not flinch. She had seen the look of disapproval that both Mr. and Mrs. Schwarz had swept over her when she arrived. She had a fine spirit in her, and did not wish to be rejected on account of physical disability. She knew that it she were rested and accustomed, she could match her strength plus her strong will against any girl, and she meant to prove it so. Hers was to be no moping, half-way service, disagreeable as her situation seemed to her at present.

Her view of the future was by no means brightened by the advent of the son of the house and the three hired men who presently obeyed the summons to supper, performing their noisy ablutions on the back porch. They were big blond men with pink complexions, whose appearance the grime of sweat and toil did not enhance. Sylvester Schwarz was lank and flabby, with a selfish mouth and a pimply face, which the sun had turned to brick color. He had small, cruel blue eyes. When Hilda made the acquaintance of the animals about the place, she found it impossible not to think of Sylvester when she glanced into the adobe of the swine. It may have been the way he cast his greedy little eyes upon her when he entered the kitchen. From the first he seemed to claim her for his prey, and from the first she had the most revolting dislike toward him. Perhaps he sensed that at the start, for the light of battle and the assurance of final victory followed hard in his face upon his first greedy glance.

The other three men were older, with stolid faces much like the master, and all had a cunning look in their eyes. She liked none of them. One, whom they called Fritz, wore a large yellow curling moustache, and his red wet lips bulged beefily between its parting. He smiled when he saw Hilda, and gave her an appraising glance that brought the blood angrily into her cheeks. His eyes were larger and bolder than the rest, and he used them much on Hilda, as she came and went from stove to table serving pork, cabbage, coffee and Limburger cheese.

She had been fiercely hungry when supper was first put upon the table, but by the time that she had finished serving the men and was free to eat what food they had left she was too dizzy and faint to care for it. The thought of the food sickened her. She did her best with a mouthful or two of bread and a swallow of coffee, but her head was aching badly before she was through with her tasks.

The men sat on the back porch, smoking, talking in loud tones, telling vile stories and laughing among themselves. Almost entirely they spoke in German. She heard one of them ask Mrs. Schwarz about her, where she came from and if she understood German, and Mrs. Schwarz told them no, she was American. The one they called Fritz laughed and said that was better, they would not have to be so careful; and she wondered idly what he meant, for it had not seemed to her they were careful in their speech either in German or English. She resolved that for the present she would not let them know that she had not only been the finest German scholar in her class in high school, but had also always kept up the practice of conversing with her father in his native tongue. It would at least give her the advantage of being left out of the conversation most of the time, and this seemed to her most desirable, in fact, the only possible way to live among them. She could not imagine herself ever having any more to do with any of them than was absolutely necessary.

She was wringing out her dishcloth and hanging it up to dry as she made these resolutions, and she did not see that Sylvester Schwarz had arisen from his seat on the back steps and lounged silently into the kitchen. Not until he was close behind her did she realize that anyone was there, and then too late. He caught her in his arms and gave her a resounding smack on her cheek.

Hilda screamed with horror, and, snatching the big wet dishcloth, whipped it smartly across his face, struggling wildly all the while, until, blinded by the dishcloth he let her go. She darted away from him and ran plump into his mother, who had rushed downstairs to see what was the matter. Hilda flung her arms around the astonished woman's neck and burst into tears.

"Ach! Vat haf you pin doing, Sylvester?" complained his mother, quite upset by Hilda's appeal, and standing helpless with the girl's arms around her unsympathetic neck. "Can't you zee she iss strange? Go vay and leef her be!"

Sylvester stood sheepishly in the middle of the floor, and Hilda caught a glimpse of the other men outside laughing at him as she raised her head from the ample, unresponsive bosom and began to realize that it was no refuge for her. She must hold her own alone against all odds in this house.

"Ach! She ain't so fine and fancy as you think,

24

Mom!" retorted Sylvester sneeringly. "You ought to seen her flirtin' with the train hands when she first come, and him a tootin' the whistle at her for the whole country to hear. She ain't so pertickiler as she tries to make out!"

Hilda flashed a look of horror and contempt at the young man and straightened up like a young rush as she turned to the woman.

"I was not flirting, Mrs. Schwarz. That engineer saved me from being run over and killed down at the junction where I changed cars. He was very kind and put me on the train and told me he would whistle when he passed this farm, and if I had found the place all right I could wave something out of the window to let him know. I am not that kind of a girl, Mrs. Schwarz!"

"Ach! Well! What's the difference! You better get to your ped. You haf to get up at half-past four. There is much to be done tomorrow!"

Blinded with tears Hilda stumbled up the stairs, dimly aware that the oldest of the three laborers, the one they called Heinrich, with gray streaks in his stubbly hair, was standing outside the door glaring angrily in at Sylvester Schwarz. She heard his contemptuous guttural hurled like a command:

"Pig! Come out o' that!" and she realized that she was being gruffly championed, but was too distraught for even a grateful glance in his direction. It was horrible to have to be championed by one so utterly repulsive.

She locked her door and dropped upon her hard little bed, terrified, despairing, exhausted. The future seemed a blackness of horror. She was too sick at heart to think if she might get away from it all. Yet how could she stay for even a night? To live in that house with all those dreadful men! To be scolded, driven, by that hard, unfeeling woman, and sworn at by the stolid husband! It seemed impossible to endure. Yet where could she go and what could she do but stay? Even supposing she succeeded in getting away without anyone noticing, she had but a dollar and ten cents in the world, and that would not carry her back to her mother. Poor Mother! How frightened she would be if she knew in what a position her young daughter had been placed! Mother thought she was to have a nice, pleasant home with friends of Uncle Otto, good Christian people who would treat her "like a daughter." "Good, kind Germans," that was what Uncle Otto had said when he got her the place. She shuddered at the thought of what it would mean to be a daughter in this house. The sting of Sylvester Schwarz's kiss was still on her cheek. She rubbed wildly at it again, and slipping from her bed, groped her way through the dark to her window. She must get away. Could she, dared she, get out of that window and steal away in the night?

She looked out in the darkness. The sky overhead was luminously kind, but far away. There was starlight and a young moon, serene but distant, unheeding of her distress. The tears rained down upon her hands, which were clasped desperately on the window sill as she knelt, her breast heaving with silent sobs she dared not make audible lest they should be heard downstairs. She put her head down on the window sill and prayed a pitiful little prayer. Heaven seemed so far away tonight. Did God care about her? She looked out again.

It seemed a long way to the ground in the darkness and very black below. She could not remember how it had appeared when she had looked out in the afternoon. She had been all taken up with watching the engineer's cap then and realizing that he had actually kept his word and whistled to her. How long ago that seemed, and how different he had been from these dreadful men among whom she had come to live. Kind, gentle, strong, courteous, gallant! She could feel his arms lifting her now, and holding her against the bars of the fence as the trains flew by on either side! Oh, that she were back at that spot in her life and could turn and flee from this new life, anywhere, so it was not here! Better even if her life had ended quickly, sharply under those fierce wheels!

She reached out her hands wistfully to the black line of the railroad grade. If his train would only pass again and she could signal her distress! But it was night! He could not see a signal if he

came. Red he had said for danger. Had she anything red? Yes, a little red scarf she had caught
up and stuffed in her suitcase just before leaving
home, because it reminded her of her school
days and all she was leaving behind. She turned
and groped in her suitcase in the darkness till she
felt the woolly softness of the scarf and hugged it
to her breast, kissing and crying over it. How
many times her mother had tied it around her
throat on a cold day, and how she had hated to
wear it sometimes as she grew older and did not
want to be bundled up. But now it was precious.
It reminded her of her mother, and of the little
brother who had often worn it also.

Sobbing softly she stumbled back to her bed
again, the old red scarf in her arms, and pulling
the stubby quilt up over her, sobbed herself to
sleep. Somehow it seemed too awful a place to
think of undressing and going to bed regularly,
but she was so utterly weary with her hard exciting day that she could stand up no longer.

Some time in the night she awoke from an ugly
dream in which she was being pursued over
plowed ground by Sylvester Schwarz, who was
determined to get her old red scarf away from
her, and her own cries for help were stifled in her
throat as she struggled on over the furrows. Off
in the distance she heard a dim rumble of a
freight train, like a kindly voice to still her fright.
It soothed and comforted her, so that she fell
asleep again.

The raucous voice of Mrs. Schwarz sounded in her ear while it was yet dark, and a vigorous shaking of her locked door brought her to her feet frightened and half stupefied with sleep.

There was no place for her to wash in her room; nothing but the tin basin on the bench by the pump below, and the roller towel on the kitchen door, which she was expected to use in common with the men who were spluttering through their ablutions now. Hilda determined to omit much of her toilet until she could beg for better accommodations for washing. If worse came to worst there was an old towel in her suitcase, and she could certainly find something in which to carry up water — that is, if she stayed here. The horror of the morning made her sure she would find some way of escape before another night if possible.

The men were cross and all swearing at each other in German. Something had happened in the night, or else it had not happened. Hilda could not quite make out from their chance remarks that floated out to the kitchen where she was frying sausage and potatoes. She was not interested and paid little heed.

Sylvester Schwarz did not come down to breakfast with the men. He slept late, and when he came his mother waited upon him and hovered over him till his father came in from the team, his little pig eyes snapping angrily, and began swearing at Sylvester like a raging bull. It seemed that the young man had been trusted with some weighty errand to a neighboring village the evening before and had neglected or forgotten it until too late. His father raged as if it were a matter of life and death. Sylvester sat stolidly, sullenly, and ate many hot cakes that his indulgent mother baked and brought to him incessantly, with silent tears running down her fat countenance. She spoke no word of protest to her angry spouse, but doggedly fed the pampered culprit till old Schwarz turned on her a storm of words that made the young girl in the kitchen cringe and heartily wish she did not understand German. During the tirade she managed to secure a basin of clean water and escape to her room till the storm was over and Sylvester gone sullenly off with a hoe over his shoulder. It appeared that Sylvester's mission had been one which called for mental attainments, for Hilda heard his father hurl this final sentence after him as he sauntered toward the barn:

"What for did I gif you all this expensive education yet if it was not to look after this end of the pizness? You will bring us all to zhame if you keep on. You might as well know nothing, you pig of a boy!"

Hilda worked silently, almost frenziedly, as the sun rose higher and the morning went on. Mrs. Schwarz moved stolidly through her domain, giving sharp commands, finding incessant fault, and growing more and more unreasonable. Just as the dinner was ready to dish up, and the men were answering the call, Hilda wiped her hands, drew down her sleeves, and turned on her fat persecutor:

"I better tell you, Mrs. Schwarz, I don't think I will stay. I'm not the kind of girl you need here. I've never had experience in heavy work, and I can see I don't suit you. I know that I can do better work in some other line and it's best for me to stop right now before you've taken a lot of trouble to teach me your ways."

Mrs. Schwarz went stolidly on dishing up the potatoes as though she had not heard. When the last potato was steaming on the piled-up dish she remarked monotonously:

"H'm! What can you do? Otto Lessing send you here. You got to stay! What else can you do?"

"Why, I thought if you could lend me the money to go back to Chicago my teacher would find me a place where I could earn enough to pay you back. I could learn stenography nights while I am working and very soon get a good position."

"Ach! I have no money! And if I had, Otto Lessing send you here, and here you stay! Unless Otto Lessing say you can go, you stay! I know you are no good to me, but what can I do? You and I are women. We must do what we are told."

Hilda stood struggling between anger and amazement, trying to think what to say. At last she answered haughtily:

"Very well, then, I will write to my Uncle Otto and tell him. If you will excuse me now, I will go up and write the letter at once. Or perhaps it would be best to send a telegram and my uncle can send me some money."

"You have no time to write letters and there is no way to send telegrams here. You get down off your high horse and carry in the potatoes! Your Uncle Otto send you here, and your time pelongs to me now. You are mighty poor help, but such as it is it pelongs to me. Take that platter in and shut up!"

This was the only result of her well-planned decision. Hilda saw she had little chance unless she made a determined stand and ran away. She looked out the back door and saw the line of rough, burly men, headed by Schwarz, coming up the path to dinner, and knew this was no time to run, so with whitening lips and trembling hands, she accepted the platter of hot stew and carried it meekly to the table, in a panic lest she would not get back to the protection of the kitchen before Sylvester arrived. She saw that for the present, at least, she must be obedient and unobtrusive, for how indeed could she run away and get anywhere without money? And it was plain there was no further use in asking Mrs. Schwarz.

All that afternoon she worked silently, doggedly, her heart raging, her mind in a turmoil. When the two o'clock freight passed and the whistle screamed its signal, her heart leaped gratefully and tears sprang to her smarting eyes, but fortunately she was scrubbing the floor with her back to Mrs. Schwarz and bore her scrutiny without a tremor. She was glad when she went up to her room to wash that she had left her towel in the window to dry. It was not large nor noticeable, but it was there; a white, silent recognition of the young man's kindness. He had said she was to let him know by this signal that she was all right! Oh, if he knew how far from right she was! If only she had thought to put the old red scarf beside the towel in the window! But, then, what could he do? He had his train to run, and when he was through with his day's work he would be far enough from her! And she was only a little stranger girl to whom he had been kind.

Nevertheless, the sound of the kindly whistle had heartened her, and she took new courage from the passing presence of her friend. After all, who was she that her way should be made smooth through life? Should she not encounter some hard places and overcome them? For the time being her lot seemed to be cast inevitably in this most unkindly spot. It was intolerable. It was inconceivable that it should be right for her to remain in such a situation long. There would be some way out of it surely. But for the moment, the day at least, until a way opened, she must be brave. She must be worthy of having had her life saved in such a remarkable way.

Surely the good God had saved her for some little purpose. It might be only that it was going to be good for her to pass through this unpleasant experience. Whatever it was, she would hold herself to win out if courage and faithfulness could do it. Perhaps the way to get away was to work hard and win the favor of these strange, disagreeable people. If they were human they must have a kinder side to them somewhere if she could only find it. Except, perhaps, that loutish son! Oh, how could she abide another day under the same roof with him? But even he might perhaps be avoided. She would do her best.

So she tried to cheer herself and scrubbed with a right good will till her young back ached and her arms, all unaccustomed to such violent exercise, began to tremble. Still, white with weariness and faint for lack of food because she had been too excited to eat, she slaved on through the afternoon work; over the hot stove, cooking the supper which she was too fatigued again to eat; thankful only that she was allowed to remain in the kitchen and cook rather than to serve at the table with those awful men. She came at last to the time when, the dishes done, she might hang up her dish towels and creep up the stairs to her room. One horror she had been spared tonight. Sylvester had taken himself off after supper, and she had not been bothered by his attentions. Heinrich, of the gray stubbly hair, had established himself ominously in the kitchen doorway and barred all approaches of any of the men. She disliked him with all her heart, but she could not but be grateful to him whatever his motive might be.

She had asked for a candle and was given a small bit grudgingly. With this flickering uncertain light, she tried to write to her mother and uncle, but before she had half finished her mother's letter the candle flickered down to the socket and went out, and her aching back and arms cried out for rest. Sleep was heavy on her eyelids, too, and she knew she had not written what she meant. Besides, it was hard, now she was at it, to tell her mother what kind of a place she was in. Supposing there was no way out. Supposing she must stay here awhile. There was no need to make her mother anxious. She had enough trouble already. No, she must write her uncle.

She groped to her window sill and with only the starlight to guide her, she scrawled a few lines to her uncle, slipped them in an envelope, sealed, addressed and stamped it, and laid it ready for mailing in the morning. Then she went to her bed.

Sleep was her master now, and she had no chance for the heavy problems she had meant to think out on her pillow. She sank at once into a deep, exhausted slumber that seemed to end almost at once with the sharp voice of her mistress in her ear and the merciless grip of duty on her tired young shoulder. She woke with the consciousness of the inevitable that had her in its power. She had heard of Prussianism, but she did not know that she was beginning to experience it.

When she went down in the morning she took her letters and asked Mrs. Schwarz how she should mail them. She was told to lay them on the table and "he" would see to them. Hilda had a feeling that they had fallen into an abyss, as from the distance of the kitchen she saw her letters swept up in the elder Schwarz's big gnarled fist. Instinctively, she felt they might never reach their destination. Surely not until they had passed the censorship of this household tyrant. She spent the day trying to devise a means by which she might mail her own letters, or at least send a telegram. She was beginning to feel virtually a prisoner on this farm.

Yet there was little time to think. She was driven from one duty to another, and the sudden violent plunge into unwonted labor had made her so stiff and sore in every joint that she could scarcely move without pain.

Three age-long days and three more nights, all too short for resting, passed, with only the sound of the friendly freight whistle to mark the daylight, and the rumble of the midnight freight through her dreams for comfort. The fourth night she cried herself to sleep once more, because the expected letter from Uncle Otto had failed to appear. The day had been so tortuous with its drudgery, so bleak in its monotony, the future seemed so impossible, so interminable, like eternity in hell. Then, suddenly, some time after midnight, she awoke with a strange insistent whirring approaching in the air through the night. It seemed to be coming on straight through the house, like some terrible destroying animal that nothing could stay, and the sound of it was like no sound that she had ever heard before. Nearer and nearer it drew, and she sprang from her bed softly and crept to her window. She could hear stealthy, sudden noises in the house, as if some other sleeper had also been aroused by the sound.

The moon was larger now, and very low. The stars were clear and there was a soft radiance over everything that made the plowed fields look like some hallowed spot. Up in the sky, not far away, from where the monster noise was coming, she saw a dark cloud-like bird of enormous proportions curve and settle and disappear somewhere in the shadows of the meadow behind the barn and the noise died away slowly into the night. Hilda rubbed her eyes and wondered if she had been dreaming.

Then out from the back of the house there passed like a wraith the form of a man and kept moving on, a shadowy speck, down the path through the cabbage patch, past the lettuce and turnips, past the barn, between the rows of tomato plants, on into the meadow. After he had disappeared, Hilda wondered if she had really seen him at all, and, shivering, crept back to bed and lay, alert, listening, with every muscle tense and every sense keen. Sometimes she thought she heard distant voices. She did not know what she thought. Her heart was beating somewhere up in her throat, and her head was aching in great hot and cold waves. It seemed as though she must keep calm and take deep breaths, or she would go out in the tenseness of the moment.

3

It was a long time she lay so, with the crooning of the frogs in the distance down by the railroad, croaking away as if nothing had happened. She had almost fallen asleep, and the beating in her throat was slowly quieting down, when the voices came again, distantly, quietly, but growing nearer. She slipped from her bed and crept once more to the window. Soft, padded steps were coming and sibilant utterances in German. They drew nearer until they were directly under her window. She kept quite still and held her breath now, and the tenseness of the strain hurt her chest, but she was not thinking of herself.

"You are quite sure we can talk here unheard?" a strange voice was saying in cultured German.

The grunt of assent in response was unquestionably from the elder Schwarz.

"Whose is that window up there? It is open."

"It is only that child they have sent down to helb in the kidgen. She does nod onderstand German. You are safe."

"Don't be too sure. It does not take long to learn a few words."

"She iss much too stupid to learn. I don'd know whad Otto Lessing means sending her here, unless he wants to ged rid of her. She iss no good to vork. You need nod pe afraid. She iss sound asleeb. Und, anyvay, she vould nod know vat you mean even if she onderstand the German. She is a child of that foolish brudder of Otto Lessing, who married an American voman. She is a sigley little thing. Can't stand nothing!"

"It is not wise to be too sure about anyone. I never trusted that Heinrich you think so much of. One cannot be too guarded. Remember, the Fatherland is depending on you. A great deal hangs on your success or failure here. There must be nothing done that would cast the slightest breath of suspicion this way. This is one of the most important stations. When France and England are subdued — and the day is not far off — all must be in readiness here, and we shall make short work of this country. The people are all asleep and can be taken without a fight, only we must look out that they do not waken before the time. Remember you are held responsible here. The All-Highest is looking to you. You must not run a single risk. Look out that your men here do not know too much! Trust them only so far as you have to. And now for your report. Did the rifles arrive safely and in good condition? Good! And you have them stored in a dry, safe place? Is that the only door? Well, if there is another inner one I would conceal this one with brush. You cannot be too careful. I would advise you to put three or four inches of earth over this trap and plant something, any small plants that can be transplanted occasionally without arousing suspicion or calling attention when it becomes necessary to open the door. Of course, we cannot tell just how soon these arms may be needed. Everything is thoroughly organized. If there should be a sudden victory abroad we could send out the order for an uprising here within twenty-four hours. You must look out that those rifles are kept in perfect condition for immediate use. And the powder and dynamite? They have come? How much! Ah! That is well. You will need to be ready to furnish it on demand with an order from your captain almost any day now. Your orders are to be on hand tomorrow to unload another consignment of potatoes and fertilizer when the car is dropped off here. Let someone guard the car, but have your wagon break down, so that you will be delayed till evening. It is better so, some stray traveler might come along and observe you. Of course, you will carry no lanterns into the car. In the front end, toward the right corner, you will find a box marked 'Turnip Seed.' Carry it carefully.

"And now I have special orders for your son. He must go up to town during this coming week and enlist in the American Army. His orders are in this envelope, and he will bring all his 'reports' here to you —"

Schwarz's voice murmured a protest, but the hard, cultured voice went on:

"It is of no use to urge such woman's foolish-

41

ness. It is the command! Is it not what you sent him to the Fatherland to be educated for, that he might serve his country? He will be in a remarkable position to obtain information which is very much needed. He should be glad he has the great honor to serve in so high a capacity. Now, will you show me where you have put the powder?"

The two men moved softly away over the grass, and their voices were audible no longer. Hilda drew a long breath and found she was trembling from head to foot. What did it all mean? Could she be dreaming?

When she scrambled out of bed the next morning in answer to the angry summons at her door the occurrences of the night came at once sharply to her mind, and she found her fingers trembling as she tried to fasten the buttons in her hasty toilet. Had it all really happened, or was it only an ugly dream? She went and looked out of her window. The sky was crimson with dawn, and the grass below her window was quite visible. There were no signs in the short young turf of recent footsteps. There was nothing to mark the place but a large iron cover with a big thick ring by which to lift it. It looked as if it might be the cover to an old cistern, or possibly a coal pit. It had not excited her curiosity when she had seen it before, but now she recalled some of the sentences spoken beneath her window, and looked again. Could this be the trap-door the stranger had spoken of? But no, it must all have been a dream, of course!

She hurried down the stairs, fastening her apron and trying to put thoughts of the night before out of her mind.

Mrs. Schwarz was putting on a clean table-cloth and making the room tidy. She had an air of suppressed excitement, and two spots on her cheeks blazed forth redder than usual. Her eyes snapped like electric sparks, and there was something about her that made Hilda hasten to the kitchen to be out of her way.

The men were more quiet than usual when they came down, and they stood about restlessly, casting furtive glances out of the door as though they awaited a superior.

Hilda had about decided that her experience of the night had been all a hallucination, when she heard voices, and glancing out saw Schwarz and a tall, well-built stranger coming out of the barn. They paused a moment, looking at something just within the door, Schwarz nodding respectful assent to some evident criticism or direction, then Schwarz closed the barn door and they came on together up the path, the stranger pointing here and there and talking as they came. Hilda hurried to put the breakfast on the table that she might escape notice, but turned from arranging the dishes just in time to see all the men give the stranger a military salute as he entered. She gave him one quick glance as she slid back to the kitchen, but she knew that he had seen her. He had a face that made you sure nothing escaped his keen glance. His eyes were blue and cold and haughty, and reminded her of an eagle she had once seen in the Zoological Gardens. He had a quantity of yellow hair, combed straight back from a retreating forehead, and a long yellow moustache, curled at the ends. She could see that the other men stood in great awe of him. Even Schwarz waited to sit down until he had taken his seat. The conversation was all in German that drifted out to the kitchen as Hilda baked great plates of hot cakes, and carried on by the stranger in the tone of a superior giving orders. Hilda caught snatches of sentences now and then as she carried the plates of cakes to the table, but she could make nothing of their import. She was always aware that the stranger was watching her, and with quick alarm she schooled herself to look "dumb" as Schwarz had reported her. By sheer force of will she kept her calm, steady color even when the stranger spoke of her to Schwarz, remarking on her good looks in bold, calculating terms that made her wish to turn and flee. She felt instinctively that he was saying these insulting things to test her knowledge of the German, and she tried to look as stupid as she could, though her blood was boiling, and her heart was thumping wildly in her breast. The ordeal of the breakfast seemed an eternity in passing, and for once she welcomed the long dishwashing that would keep her in the kitchen out of view.

Even here, however, she was not safe. She heard footsteps behind her, and, with a growing consciousness of being watched, looked up to see the stranger standing silently by her, watching her like a big cat waiting to spring on a mouse. As her eyes met his a half-cynical smile began to dawn on his face:

"What is your name, my pretty one?"

The question was asked in his perfect German, with just the touch of contemptuous patronage that one gives to an inferior. Almost she forgot herself and lifted her chin haughtily. But just in time her part came to her and she simply stared at him a second uncomprehendingly and went on with her dishwashing, splashing around in the soapy water without regard to his fine coat; and quite naturally, as she had hoped he would do, he stepped back.

Then, horrified at Hilda's presumption, out came Mrs. Schwarz, with angry brows and mortified apologies:

"She doesn't understand the German, Captain. You'll have to excuse her; she's awful dumb, und she don't know no petter. Hilda, the gentleman is asking your name. Can't you answer him civilly? And for mercy's sake schtop splashing him with that dirty vater!"

Hilda, with well-feigned calmness, lifted her eyes indifferently to the man's face, then turned deliberately toward her mistress and answered quietly:

"You will tell him, please, Mrs. Schwarz, that I am Miss Lessing."

Then she dropped her eyes and went on with her dishwashing, far from feeling the calmness she would have had them think she felt.

The young German stared at her in amazement for a moment, then threw his head back and laughed. But beyond a faint pink stealing into her cheeks there was no change in the gentle dignity of the girl, though she was maintaining herself by the utmost strain of nerve and will. She felt that if she were to break down now she would never be able to protect herself against something indefinable, which was, nevertheless, very real in the atmosphere of this strange house.

She succeeded well in convincing the man that she did not understand his language. But the fineness of her was something she could not hide, not at least with her inexperience. Had she but known it, she aroused his interest far more by her gentle dignified bearing than ever she would have done if she had laughed and joked with him. He might then have gone his way and cast never a thought back to her. But it would have been as impossible for Hilda to have laughed and joked with such a man as for a flower to masquerade as an onion.

He had his laugh out now, Mrs. Schwarz joining in with a polite, bewildered cackle, but he stopped suddenly with a frown and watched the girl as she went quietly on with her work, as seemingly shut away from these two as if she had been deaf and dumb and blind. A creature of exquisite fashioning in a world of her own. Her indifference piqued his dominating spirit and made him long to subdue her to himself; to crush this beautiful dignity of maidenhood and force her to bow to him as super-man.

"She is very beautiful and absurdly proud, but I find her amusing," he said to Mrs. Schwarz, and then in a tone as if he were lightly bargaining for her soul, he added lazily: "Just have it understood that she belongs to me! You understand? I may come soon again."

Then he turned to Hilda and, in beautiful English, with all the outward courtesy of a gentleman, said:

"I will bid you good morning, *Miss Lessing!*"

In dumb amazement she stood and watched him go down the path to the barn where Schwarz and two of the other men were working over a great coil of wire. Somehow in the instant of his going it came to her like a shock: *That man is a spy!*

Over and over she said it to herself as she watched him standing in the sunshine, saw the immediate attitude of salute and deference of the other two as he drew near; remembered snatches of the conversation she had overheard the night before, and took in the whole thing as a revelation.

That man is a spy! They are, perhaps, all spies!

She stood rooted to the spot where he had left her, washing and rewashing the spider in which she had cooked his sausages, and taking in the awful thought. The horror and indignation with which she had listened to his audacious and insulting order to Mrs. Schwarz concerning her were for the moment forgotten in the amazing conviction that she had discovered a spy!

Somehow her senses seemed racing around in her body in a frenzy, and she was almost blind and breathless with trying to stop them long enough to think what it all meant. So she stood and rewashed that old greasy spider till Mrs. Schwarz's rasping voice shivered on her suffering consciousness with a thrill of pain:

"How long are you going to stand there and wash that dish, you lazy girl? Get you up the stairs and make those peds, and be quig about id!" she shouted. Hilda caught her breath and hurriedly finished her dishes.

Upstairs by herself, with a view out the open windows, she saw the stranger ordering everyone about. She came to herself again and began to boil with rage over the awful thing that man had dared to say about her! She *belong* to *him!* Indeed! She would rather die a thousand deaths than belong to him. She loathed and feared him with every atom of her fine sensitive being. She was convinced without knowledge or need of proof that he was a spy, a traitor to his country and a man to be despised.

And he was coming back again! Oh, horror! Somehow she must get away before he came! She must not stay in this house another day!

It came to her that he was not yet gone. He might return to the house again. She could see him standing now between the cabbage plants, pointing to the little tool house made of bricks with an iron door. Then there flashed across her mind what he had said about the powder house. Powder and dynamite! Why should they need such things on a truck farm? She had always connected them with a red flag and blasting on a city street. But powder here! What did it mean? Where did they keep it? Surely not down in that hole with the iron trap-door below her bedroom window. They wouldn't put such things near enough to a house to blow it up! The tool house! It looked too small to hide much. It was little more than a wart on the side of a bunchy hill with young corn growing all about it. The barn? It was very large, but did they ever keep such things in a wooden building? Was that one reason why the barn was always locked? Why Schwarz was so angry at Sylvester once for leaving the door ajar?

Hilda shuddered at thought of the peril that might be all about her. She shuddered again as the sharp voice of the woman below stairs called her. She was peeling potatoes in the kitchen and her mistress was busy making pies at the kitchen table when she heard the strange whirring noise again that had so startled her in the night. She jumped and dropped a potato back into the pan again, looking up at Mrs. Schwarz with wide eyes:

"Oh, *what* is that?"

"How should I know? Attend to your work!" the woman answered crossly.

But Hilda's eyes were fixed on the open window, for out of the meadow behind the barn there arose a large, bird-like structure, skimming the air, and floating upward as lightly and easily as a mote in a sunbeam.

"Why! That must have been — !" Hilda began breathlessly, then caught her breath and changed her sentence. "Why! That *is* an *aeroplane!* I have seen them sometimes far up over Chicago. But never so close. But an aeroplane out here in the country! How did it come, Mrs. Schwarz?"

There was no answer and, turning, the girl saw that the woman stood absently gazing out of the window, a look of woe on her face and tears streaming down her cheeks.

4

Hilda's heart was touched instantly. Springing toward her mistress she cried:

"Mrs. Schwarz, you are *crying!* Is something dreadful the matter? Oh, I am so sorry!" and she timidly put her arm about the stout shoulder that, since the words of sympathy, had begun to shake with sobs. There was something terrible in seeing this great bulk of a woman with her sharp tongue and stolid ways all broken up crying.

"It iss my *poy!*" she wailed into her apron. "They vill send him avay to var! My only poy! Und there iss no need. He iss too young, and I know he vill get into drubble. He vas exempt. Ve got him exempt on accound of the farm, und now the orders haf come from the Fatherland, und he must go!"

"But what has the Fatherland got to do with him?" asked Hilda puzzled. "This is America. We are Americans. Why don't you tell the Fatherland you don't want him to go?"

Hilda's heart sank within her at the thought of keeping Sylvester at home; nevertheless, she was touched by the poor woman's grief.

But the woman her head and wiped her eyes despairingly.

"It iss no use!" she sighed. "Ve must do as the

Fatherland orders. Ve are Germans. They know pest!"

Suddenly the voice of Schwarz boomed forth just outside the door. His wife turned as if she had been shot and bolted up the stairs. Hilda had sense enough to finish her potatoes without a sign that anything unusual had just been going on, but her mind was in a turmoil over the strange and dreadful things which were constantly being revealed to her. What did it all mean, anyway? How should the Fatherland reach out to free America and presume to order what free Americans should do? And *why* should they want men to go into an army with whom they were at war? A great light suddenly broke upon her understanding as she sat staring out into the brilliant blue of the sky where only a few moments ago the great aeroplane had become a mere speck and vanished out of sight. There certainly was something queer about this place, and she must get out of it just as quickly as possible. She wished with all her heart she had taken warning from the few light words the nice young engineer had said about spies and turned about then and there. But how absurd! She had no money with which to return. And where would she have gone? Her mother had already been hurried off to Wisconsin to take charge of the orphans, and Uncle Otto would have been very angry to have her return before she had even been to the place where he sent her. Of course,

Uncle Otto did not realize what this place was like, or he never would have sent her. He would not want her to stay, and, of course, he would send her money to come back when he got her letter. But, oh, even a day or two was long to wait!

She began to wonder whether she had made her case strong enough in the letter. Uncle Otto would have no patience with suspicions. And yet she could scarcely have told more without writing a very long letter, and for that she had not had time. But perhaps she ought to write again to hurry matters. She would mail the letter herself this time to make it sure.

Mr. and Mrs. Schwarz were still talking angrily in the room overhead. Hilda gave a quick glance out the door. The men were all in the field working. She could identify each one. She slipped softly up the stairs and locked herself into her room. Then, with hurried fingers, she wrote a penciled appeal:

Dear Uncle Otto:

Won't you please, please send me money by telegraph, or at least by return mail, to come home? I cannot possibly stay here any longer. There is something very queer about this place and the people. I haven't time to tell you now, but when I come home I will explain. I am sure you would not want me to stay if you knew all about it. There are a lot of dreadful men here, and I am frightened I hope you won't be angry with me, and I hope you will send me the money at once. I can get a place to work and pay it back to you. Please hurry!

> *Your affectionate niece,*
> *Hilda Lessing*

Hastily addressing the letter she slipped it into her blouse and stole silently down the stairs again. A glance out the door showed the men still at work in the distance. She sped down the path toward the station as if on the wings of the wind. There would be a letter box at the station, of course.

It never occurred to Hilda until she reached the station and mailed her letter that she would be in full view of Mrs. Schwarz's bedroom window, but when, after a hasty glance at the deserted little shanty of a station, noting that there was no sign of agent or telegraph office, she turned to come back, she suddenly became aware of two faces framed in the upper window of the house. Not anxious to anger her employer she quickened her steps, running as nimbly as possible over the rough ground, reaching the kitchen door without delay. But to her unspeakable dismay she saw Schwarz standing there glaring out at her, his whole big frame filling the doorway, his face red and angry, the odor of liquor about him.

"Where you pin?" he snarled.

A frightened little smile of apology trembled out on Hilda's white lips:

"I've just been down to mail a letter that I wanted to have go this morning. It didn't take me a minute. I mustn't trouble you every time I have a letter to mail," she explained.

"You don't go down to that station mitout permission! You onderstandt?" he thundered.

"Oh, very well," said Hilda, dropping her lashes with a dignified sweep, though she was trembling with indignation and terror. There was something about the whole domineering make-up of Schwarz that made her think of a mailed fist.

Schwarz, with something akin to a growl, stood aside to let her pass in and she fled upstairs to her room, where she stayed behind a locked door until she heard him go down the path to the station. Her heart was fluttering wildly, and tears of bitterness were on her cheeks. It was some minutes before she could calm herself enough to return to the kitchen.

She had been at work not more than five minutes when she saw through the open door that Schwarz was striding back over the furrows to the house. Her instinct was to flee again, but the peremptory commands of Mrs. Schwarz about putting on the vegetables for dinner held her to her post.

There was something belligerent in Schwarz's attitude as he entered the kitchen and strode over to the stove. In his hand he carried an open letter and he gave her a vicious look as he opened the stove lid and stuffed the letter in, shutting down the lid again and striding out.

Hilda lifted her hands from the water in which she had been washing the cabbage and looked after him in sudden alarm. Then she sprang to the stove and lifted the lid. A flame rushed up to meet the draught and enveloped the paper, but not before she had read the words: "Dear Uncle Otto"; and "There is something strange about this place."

Trembling, she shut down the stove lid and a great despair seized her. She was then a prisoner in this house so far as any hope of writing to her friends for help was concerned! Mr. Schwarz had opened the post box and taken out her letter and read it! He had dared to do that! He did not intend that she should write any complaints to her friends. But how did he get the box open? She was sure it was a regular post office letter box such as they always have at stations. Of course, he might have been appointed station master. He probably was, as there did not seem to be any other official there. But it was a state's prison offense to open a letter! Didn't he know that? She had learned that when she was a very little girl. But perhaps he knew he had her in his power and did not care. Already she felt the iron grip of the hand that ruled this desolate household. One look in his eye was enough to know he was not troubled by any law of courtesy or kindness, or any sense of what was due to women under his protection. Protection! What a farce that word seemed when applied to him, with his little pig eyes and his cruel jaw. The cold truth slowly sank into her soul. She was in a terrible situation and there was no connection with the outside world. She must work her way out somehow and get away. The conviction that it would be no easy task and that there was a long, strong hand concealed about this farm somewhere that could and would reach out to bring her back if she attempted to run away; and that then her fate would be worse than at present, kept her from crying out and running through the open door at once, away down the track to the freedom of the world. Some intuition taught her that if she would elude these terrible people, people who were somehow mysteriously connected with the great German nation now at war with the United States, that she must not anger them nor let them suspect that she was aware of their attitude toward her. She must act out the stupidity that they now believed of her. It had been bad that Mr. Schwarz had discovered that she thought there was something strange about this place. He would begin to watch her. He would think she was not so stupid as she had at first seemed, and would perhaps set the men to guarding the house lest she escape. At any rate, she could not escape by daylight, that was certain. She must have time to think and plan. She had enough knowledge of the world to know that a girl alone without money and friends was in frightful danger. She must not move until she thought out every detail. Meantime, she must be meek and innocent and go about her work.

So she stilled her frightened heart as she heard Mrs. Schwarz come heavily down the stairs, and went briskly about her work. There was something strange about the atmosphere of the place, something intangible that got hold of the inmates. Hilda felt it. It gripped her and kept her from rebelling, kept her silent under the scathing tongue of her mistress; made her efface herself when the men came into the house. It seemed to hang about in the air and give her a helpless feeling that she must succumb — that nothing could help her out of this, that she was only a woman against a great power. Hilda had never felt anything like it before. She was a spirited girl and had ideas of her own, but now she felt as if they were gradually being paralyzed, and she would be compelled to let her will lie inert while she did the will of these stony-hearted people. Something in her struggled wildly against this state of things, but she was kept so busy that she had no time to think; and when the work was done bodily weariness was so great that she could not plan a way out of things; and so several days passed with no let-up and no hope. A strange non-resistance to the inevitable was stealing over her. Sometimes as she was dropping off to sleep she would know that if she could only be rested enough she could rise above this and plan a way out. There was just one thing she waited for and that was the end of the month, when she might hope to get her wages, and then she could quietly take her leave. She had not been told how much her wages were to be, but they would surely be enough to take her back to Chicago, or at least to some town where she could get a decent place to stay until she could find work. Sometimes, as she was going about her work, she would try to plan how little she could get along with, and once she summoned courage to ask Mrs. Schwarz how much she was earning a week, but the woman only stared with an ugly laugh and said:

"I know nodding about it. Zumetimes I think you do nod earn your salt."

And with that she went out of the room.

Hilda thought about it awhile and concluded that Mr. Schwarz managed all those matters, so that night she went to him.

"Vages!" he roared. "I pay you no vages! It iss enough that I give you a good home. You should pe thankful for that! You are not worth vages!"

Hilda, with flaming cheeks, opened her mouth to protest, to say that Uncle Otto had told her there would be good wages, but when she looked into the fierce, cunning eyes of the man, her very soul quaked. Something that would have protested two weeks before had crumpled up within her and she saw herself precipitately retiring to the kitchen from the roaring of his angry tongue.

That night when she tried to sleep she kept thinking that it was men like Schwarz who had gone to war. It was such men that the American soldiers would have to fight! She shuddered in her dreams as she thought of the long lines of gallant young soldiers she had watched marching in procession in Chicago. They had merry tunes on their lips and smiles on their faces. They walked with strength and sturdiness; but they would have to face men like Schwarz! Would the same lethargy steal over them when they got within German power as had come to her soul since she came to the truck farm to live?

She must rouse herself to do something. If only there were just one friend. There was that strong young engineer. If he only knew her plight! But it had been seven long days since his whistle had sounded out its clear blasts, three long and two short, about two o'clock every day, and waked the echoes in the valley. Perhaps he was sick, or his route had been changed, or perhaps he had gone to war like so many brave boys. She sighed as she thought of it all, so much beautiful manhood going out to meet — what? Millions of men like Schwarz! Oh, it was terrible!

It was lonelier than ever without that whistle. Of course, she had known all along that it would not last forever. He would grow tired of whistling to a stranger whom he had seen but once. It had been good to feel that there was at least one in the neighborhood who remembered her and greeted her once a day. But that was visionary. He had grown tired and he had forgotten. Of course, that was it. He had forgotten! She must never think of him any more. So she put the little red scarf away in her suitcase, for of what use would it be to hang out a signal when there was no eye to see? And she folded her neat white towel and hung it over the back of a chair in lieu of a towel rack, firmly resolving it should hang out of the window no more.

And then, it was that very next day, just at five minutes past two, that the afternoon freight came racketting down the road and the whistle sounded forth in clear cheerful blasts:

———— ! ———— ! ———— ! —— ! —— !

She was carrying a great pan of sour milk across the kitchen to Mrs. Schwarz at the time, and she started so that the milk slopped over on the clean kitchen floor and brought forth a reproof of unusual strength from the mistress.

The color flamed into Hilda's cheeks and a glad light came in her eyes. Somehow a sense of more security stole over her, and almost a little song came to lips as she went about her work. Almost, but not quite, for Mrs. Schwarz was not far away, and the men were working near the house and constantly coming back and forth.

When she went up to her bed that night she did not feel quite so disheartened as she had for the last lonely week. It was ridiculous, she told herself, that a whistle should do that to her, but it did, and she could not afford just now to put by any source of comfort.

It was that night that she was awakened again sharply, and sat up in bed with fear in her heart, and the strange whirring sound in her ears. This time she knew what it was instantly, and her hand fluttered to her throat in her horror. The air-man had returned!

Stiff and cold with fright, she crept noiselessly from her bed over to the window and dropped tensely down beside the window sill. She must find out if he was going to remain in the morning. If there was a possibility of that she must escape before dawn. She would not risk his presence again. She trembled at the thought of his repulsive eyes upon her. He filled her with loathing and a fear that she could not analyze.

After a long time she heard soft footfalls on the grass below and guarded whispers growing gradually into distinct low tones. They were talking about a very particular piece of work that must be done on the morrow. Most careful directions were given by the air-man. Certain stones in some bridge were to be drilled, certain other stones removed, so many pounds of dynamite were to be ready —. Hilda could make nothing of it at first, but suddenly something was said that made her sure that it was the great stone railroad bridge out there in the valley that they were talking about, and she sat and listened with all her soul. Gradually she began to understand from their talk that a trainload of powder and munitions was expected to be sent over that bridge soon, en route to France, and that they were planning to blow up the whole thing — bridge, munitions and all. She could not make out though she listened intently, what time this train was expected to pass, but gathered that it was a special train, and that the time would be announced by telephone later. She wondered at that, for she had nowhere seen a sign of a telephone since she came to the farm.

It also appeared that this was but the first of a series of explosions and disasters that were planned to hinder the United States in their war preparations. The visitor handed Schwarz a small piece of paper on which he said was a list of the other plots with their dates, and for which Schwarz was to prepare and collect and deal out the explosives. He told Schwarz to give it to a man named Eisel when he came. Then Schwarz stooped and lifted the big ring in the iron lid under the window, pulled up the lid, turned on his flash torch and disclosed a rude staircase down which the two men disappeared.

They were gone a long time, and Hilda sat shivering and staring into the darkness, trying to take in the colossal horror that had just been re-vealed in her hearing. She was then truly in the midst of spies! She had only half believed her own dawning convictions before. The words of the young engineer, spoken lightly, had come true!

Hot and cold waves of fear rolled from her heart to her throat and back again. A cold perspiration broke out over her whole body. Now and then a metallic clink came distinctly to her ears from the hole in the ground where the two men had disappeared. It seemed a long blank period of awfulness that she knelt there shivering in the chill of the dawning till she heard at last the low voices of the men resuming. Schwarz dropped the iron lid into place with a thud and they turned away.

"Better get your men to work at once! It's safer working before daylight," said the low voice of the stranger. "Remember to keep under cover when the trains go by. Don't take any chances. *This must go through!* Those are the orders! I'll phone you as early as possible, in code, of course. I must hurry away, and you've no time to lose. Make haste! By the way, don't forget to cover that trap-door. Better do it right away!"

The stranger made a quick salute in the darkness and hurried away down the path between the cabbages. In a moment more the whirr of his motor filled the air, and she saw a dark shape arising from the field beyond the barn. It became a speck for an instant, then disappeared.

Schwarz went stealthily into the house and tiptoed up the stairs. If she had not been on the alert she would not have known he was moving about. Someone else moved softly in the room next to hers, and by and by she saw two dark figures emerge from the shadow of the house and drift off down through the meadow toward the railroad. They carried picks and shovels, and one of them was Schwarz. She knew him by his bulky walk. They climbed the fence and were presently out of sight in the thick growth of alders by the creek.

Hilda crept back to bed and covered herself, head and all, with the quilt, shivering and trying to get warm. Her very spirit seemed frozen within her. Her world had gone cold and terrible! To think that men would plot to do such things! But she could not think. Her very thoughts seemed paralyzed. By and by, as the warmth began to creep over her, her senses seemed to return. She realized that it was America, her United States, that was being plotted against. All the days in school when she had spelled out stories of George Washington and Abraham Lincoln; all the holidays and festivals when she had marched in processions, in primary, grammar and high schools; carried flags, scattered flowers, sung songs of liberty, passed in quick review before her; the patriotic compositions and themes she had written, the poems she had recited, seemed crying out together to be heard; and the "Star Spangled Banner," with its thrilling "Oh, say, can you see!" floated all about her as if all these former evidences of her patriotism had come back in a panic over what was happening and were beseeching her to do something about it. It came to her like a revelation that she was probably the only person in the world who could do anything about it, because she was likely the only loyal one who knew about it. It was a terrible responsibility to be the only one in the world who could save many lives and great properties! And if she should fail! *If she should fail! She must not fail!* She must do something to save that bridge, and to save those other places. Steel works and shipyards and oil tanks and munition factories were all in danger! If only she knew where they were and the dates! She clasped her hands and prayed earnestly: "Oh, God, please show me what to do."

She had decided when she first heard that air-man's voice below her window that as soon as they were gone she would make up a small bundle of things, get out of her window and steal away before it was light. But she no longer had any such thought. Things were changed. She had forgotten her own plight. Her country was in peril and she must stay and find a way to help. She hadn't an idea of what she would do yet, but she was very certain she would kind a way. All the lethargy of her mind seemed gone. All the weariness and aching of her limbs were forgotten. The days of hard work and sharp words, the nights of tossing on her hard little bed were as if they had not been. She felt young and strong and alive. She was not afraid. Something dearer and bigger than herself was at stake. She was living in a house with spies; very well, she would be a spy, too! She would be an American spy!

She slipped softly from her bed and began to dress rapidly. She had no definite idea of what she was going to do yet, but the first thing was to be ready.

When she was dressed she took the little red scarf and pinned it to the window sill over her towel, where it would show bright against the white. It was ridiculous, of course, but it made her feel more comfortable just to think of it there. He might never see it — what could he do if he did? — he had his train to take on to the end of the route; but she had set her signal as he told her to if she discovered spies.

As she leaned out of her window to make sure the scarf hung free and smooth she noticed something white on the ground below. The dawn was growing in the east now, and when she looked intently she could see quite distinctly the outline of a bit of white paper. It had not been there the night before, she was sure, for she had been looking out just before she went to bed and thinking how nice it would be if there were some flowers planted down there for her to look at sometimes, and to breathe their fragrance at night. This must be something the air-man dropped. Would it be anything of importance?

Might it somehow help her to know what to do?

But how was she to get it! She dared not risk going down after it. Mrs. Schwarz would be sure to hear her. She could hear her up and moving about now in her heavy bare feet in her room across the hall. If Hilda's door should open she would call out at once to know why she was up so early without being called. No, she must not arouse suspicion. Perhaps there would be time after she got down to the kitchen to run around the house and pick up the paper, but not likely after Mrs. Schwarz was down. She would be cross and exacting and the men always swarmed everywhere early in the morning. Besides, some-one might miss it by that time and hunt it up. Also she might leave tracks in the dewy grass if she ran around the house. No, there ought to be some way for her to get that paper without going downstairs. What could it be? She measured the distance between the window and the ground, examining the window ledge and the smooth side of the house. There was no possibility of climbing down and up again, for even if she reached the ground without a mishap how could she get up again? She canvassed the possibility of tying her bedclothes together and making a rope by which to descend, trying to pull herself up again, but that was too much of a risk. She might get caught midway and then there was no know-ing what they might do to her; but certainly they would see to it that she had no further chance of showing her loyalty to the United States. No, she must not risk climbing down.

Was there anything she could let down, a bent pin or a hat pin thrown down hard enough to make it go through the paper and pull it up? No, it would slip off before she could draw it up. Her open umbrella? Would it be possible to let it down and sweep up the paper?

She cast an anxious glance toward the sky. The glow was spreading in the east and it would soon be light. There was no telling how soon Schwarz and his companion would return across the meadow and an umbrella traveling up and down the side of the house would be a noticeable object. Besides, it might catch and bump and make a noise against the wall. There were open windows all about. Once sound an alarm and all would be lost. If there were only some small object with sticking plaster on it: something to which the paper would adhere! If she only had a bottle of mucilage or glue she might smear it on something and let it down. The paper was almost beneath the window. Why hadn't she brought with her that little tube of photograph paste instead of giving it to her brother? Was there nothing, *nothing* she could use? Must she let that paper go uninvestigated when it might contain something of great importance to the country?

She got up and went softly about her room in the dim light, feeling of article after article on the small box that constituted her dressing table and her hand came upon her tube of toothpaste. She drew in her breath exultantly. The very thing! Would the paper stick to it? She would try. She would have to put it on something heavy enough to press the stickiness into the paper and make it adhere. Her hair brush? No, the flat side would not drop down easily. She must have something with a flat bottom. Her ink bottle! That would do.

It was some minutes before she could find strings enough to reach from her window to the ground, but by means of tape and bits of ribbon she at last had her strange fish-line ready, firmly fastened around the neck of the bottle, the other end tied to a chair lest some hasty move should cause her to drop it and she have one more article to fish up. Then she smeared the bottom of the ink bottle generously with toothpaste.

It was growing light now. She knelt breathlessly by the window and slowly played out her line, steadying the ink bottle as it went down to keep it from whirling wide and knocking against the house. She was trembling from head to foot when the bottle with a final whirl settled down firmly on the paper. For a full minute she let it rest there to make the paste stick and then, with heart beating so loud she felt as if the people in the house must hear it she began slowly to pull the line up, hand over hand. There was a tense moment when the bottle lifted from the ground and the paper wavered slightly as if debating whether it would go or stay. Then it rose steadily with the bottle, inch by inch, until it was within her reach and she put her hand out and grasped it.

Carefully she wiped off the toothpaste and eagerly scanned the writing. It was in German, interspersed with hieroglyphics. It meant nothing whatever to her:

"Remington, Du Pont, Eddystone, Carnegie, Chester Ship Building —."

Some of the names were indicated by strange marks. There were dates and words that she could not understand. Her face fell in disappointment. There was no help here for the task before her. Almost she flung the hard-won paper back to the ground. Then she remembered it was stained with toothpaste and might betray her. A second thought also reminded her that some wiser head than her own might make something important out of it.

Hastily wrapping it in a clean handkerchief, she fastened it firmly inside her blouse and prepared to respond to Mrs. Schwarz's call to work.

As Hilda threw open the kitchen window by the sink she caught a glimpse of a man disappearing into the door of the little brick hut down the garden path, and a moment later while she stood in the same place filling the teakettle with fresh water she had another fleeting glimpse of a figure in brown jeans, crouched and stealthily stealing out of the door again and down among the bushes carrying something under his left arm. It was all so brief in the dim light of the morning that she was not at all certain whether the man was Heinrich or one of the others, but her thoughts lingered about the little brick hut and she kept a furtive watch for more comings and goings. Several happenings of late had made her sure that the little brick hut was the home of the powder and dynamite that the man of the night had mentioned in his visits. Somehow she felt as if the Great War which until a few days ago had seemed a mere incident of history, so far away and unreal, had suddenly flung its whole terrible problem at her trembling feet, and the fate of the world lay in her hands.

5

The very atmosphere seemed fraught with suppressed excitement that morning. Mrs. Schwarz was in the worst of moods. Hilda wondered if she, too, were in the secret, but decided not when she saw how angry she was at Schwarz for not coming to breakfast on time. Later, when Sylvester slouched sullenly down to his morning repast and the mother crooned about him tearfully, she discovered that her perturbation was due to the fact that her son was to leave her that morning for the dread enlistment, and Mrs. Schwarz had no mind or eyes for anything else.

"You vill pe killed! I know you vill pe killed!" complained the woman and sat staring at the unhandsome selfish piece of flesh that was her son, with eyes of despair, and a hopeless droop to her mouth.

"Oh, rot! Shut up, can't you?" growled the son ungraciously. "It's bad enough to have to go without hearing you go on about it!" and he helped himself to another pork chop and allowed his mother to pour him another cup of coffee. Hilda, in the midst of her tumult of mind, rejoiced with a passing relief that the young man was to leave, for although he had not annoyed her openly since the night when Heinrich had defended her there was still a covert fire in his eye when he looked her way that made her always afraid to be left alone in his vicinity.

Sylvester left on the ten o'clock train amid the silent weeping of his mother. None of the men had come to breakfast yet, but ten minutes later the two younger ones came in from the lower part of the garden and sat down to be served. Hilda wondered how they could have been working down there and she not have seen them before; but later when they went back to their work she watched them closely and saw that they only made a detour through the lower part of the garden and dropped away behind the bushes that surrounded the creek. She saw their hats appear once or twice lower down the valley toward the bridge. Were they hiding their tracks in the stream?

She looked across at the great stone bridge spanning the valley, as strong and gray and massive as the rock itself that cropped out of the mountain, and looking as much a part of the scenery as if it had grown there from the foundation of the world. It seemed incredible that any human being would lay the hand of destruction upon it, would dare to destroy it — or could. It seemed impossible. And yet, she had heard the words clearly under her window, and there were the men at work. They had come back for tools, perhaps. What kind of a looking thing was dynamite? She had heard of it as sticks and balls, but those might only be technical terms. She had never paid much attention to such things, and had not ever asked any questions about explosives. She had a shuddering horror of the subject generally. And now here was this great catastrophe apparently going to be pulled off before her very eyes and she the only one who had knowledge of it to prevent it — she was powerless.

She looked furtively across the dining-room to the stolid woman who sat staring out of the door toward the station where her son had departed, weak tears running down the little anxious gutters in her fat cheeks and neck. She looked repulsive, like Sylvester, as she sat so, with her mouth half open in a pitiful suppressed sob. Hilda decided that she did not know of the work going on at the bridge or if she did it was nothing to her. Perhaps in a general way she knew they were here on this desolate farm for some purpose. Perhaps this was a regular nest of spies and she was part of it — she, Hilda Lessing, who had held the big flag in the spring celebration and been at the head of the high school lines as they marched in procession through the streets of Chicago with the whole city swarming close and cheering while they sang the "Star Spangled Banner" — she, to be mixed up with spies, and implicated in this terrible crime! The thought of her own peril came for the first time and sent hot prickles over her flesh, but a wave of patriotism swept all thought of herself away. The bridge *must not be destroyed!* She must do something to save it. But when? How?

She looked again at the old woman, weeping and oblivious in her doorway. Now was as good a time as any to run away and tell somebody and stop this horror before it happened! She could slip unseen around the house and into the bushes on the other side of the track and make the station without Mrs. Schwarz seeing her. There usually was a train about this hour, and it mattered not which way it was going so she got away. She had only a dollar, but she could ride as far as that took her and then telephone to the President at Washington. Perhaps he would know something to do to save the bridge before it was too late. After that she surely could find some place to work until she earned enough to get to her mother. Anyway, she must try, for she could not let such a terrible thing happen and lives be lost perhaps as well as property, and not try to do something.

She lifted her hands from the dishwater and wiped them on her apron, wondering if she dared risk it to go up to her room for her hat. Perhaps Mrs. Schwarz would hear her and be roused from her stupor of grief. It was well she always kept her bit of money in its little bag around her neck. She would not have to go without that. She turned, deciding that flight was best while the going was good, and then suddenly a shadow darkened the doorway of the kitchen and her heart stood still with fright.

Schwarz loomed before her, his face like a cyclone, his hands and garments grimed with clay, his trousers wet to the knees, his boots caked with red mud.

"I have lost some valuable paper!" he roared. "I must find it before the man comes ad noondime. Haf you ben round the hauze dis morning, you?" and he pointed his finger at Hilda with a menacing jab.

Hilda trembled and she felt the burning of the paper over her heart, but she shook her head and tried to look apathetic.

"You zure?"

She shook her head again.

"Vell, then, you sdop vat you do und go hunt mit me. I mide uv tropped it on de stairs."

"What sort of paper was it?" Hilda asked, wondering if it were really the missing paper that crackled under her blouse whenever she moved.

"Shust a paper mit wriding on it. 'Pout zo pig!" and he measured with his hands.

Hilda, conscious of the likeness, turned to hide her face in the dark stairway, and lighting a match went on her search. Below she could hear the roar of the angry man like a beast enraged, and the placating whine of his gloomy wife.

"I *bust* haf it!" he cried. "I tell you I *bust haf it* pefore de messenger comes. It vas de list for him. Derc iss no udder. *No!* I do not remember! I did not read id. I did nod haf time! I haf ben bizzy zince. You haf pin gareless. I know you haf! You are sudge a fool apout dat poy going avay! You alvays vas a fool! All vimen are fools!" His voice bellowed all over the house, and Hilda could fairly see the cringing meekness of his sad, fat wife as she roused herself to help him.

He went cursing off down toward the barn, and Mrs. Schwarz, now thoroughly aroused, took up the storm of rage and visited it upon Hilda. She sent the girl looking through all the papers in the trash basket and herself went mauling through a liner in the big old desk in the corner of the dining-room. Presently she appeared in the kitchen door with a piece of paper.

"You run town and dake this to him qvick. I dink dis iss de ride vun!" she said.

Hilda did not relish the task, but there was nothing for it but to obey. She took the paper and hurried down the path, glancing at it as she went, wondering if perhaps she ought to somehow hide it, too, if it proved to be the list. But no, it was only a list of garden seeds written out, so many bushels of potatoes, so much seed corn and lettuce and cabbages. If it were some queer code, perhaps she could at least remember the articles, and she glanced over them again as she hurried along to the barn, resolved to write them down as soon as she got back to the house, and tell somebody about it as soon as she could get away.

That she might the more clearly fix the words

in order on her mind's eye, she slowed her gait just a trifle, and so she came near to the barn and heard Mr. Schwarz talking loudly, violently, pausing and talking again as if he were answering somebody.

"You did not give it to me at all!" she heard in German, excitedly. "I am sure you did not!"

Then Hilda pushed open the door and stepped inside holding up the paper, saying: "Is this the paper you are looking for, Mr. Schwarz?"

She stopped, astonished. Schwarz was talking over the telephone! So this was where it was hidden! Down in the corner of a dusty, cluttered barn, behind an old reaper!

But Schwarz turned at her voice and hung up the receiver with a click of rage.

"Got oud of dis!" he yelled, shaking his fist at her. "Got oud of dis! Who told you you could come indo dis parn? You fool! You idiot! You —"

Then he clutched at the paper she held and with his other hand shoved her roughly from the barn and closed the door. An instant he paused in his rage to glance at the paper, then tore it in pieces and raised his hand as if to strike her. Hilda sped away up the path and back to the kitchen, watching anxiously from the window till Schwarz went back into the barn again, this time taking the precaution to close and lock the door behind him. Hilda's heart was beating wildly. She put her hands back at their dishwashing while she tried to think what to do. Should she risk running away in plain sight of Mrs. Schwarz with her husband near enough to call, and doubtless the other men not too far away to hear a signal and give chase, or should she wait a little while in the hope that Schwarz would go back to the valley again?

Schwarz came out of the barn again presently, but he did not return to the house. Instead, he lurched down to the little brick hut, went in a minute, and came out again to sneak around among the bushes and disappear.

Now was her chance. She would wait till Mrs. Schwarz went out of the kitchen again and then she would take flight. This was no place for her to stay longer. The man would have struck her if she had not been quicker than he and got out of his way.

But Mrs. Schwarz did not go out of the kitchen. She seemed to have decided to visit upon Hilda all that had been put upon herself. She stormed around the kitchen and demanded that the girl should do this and that, called her from one duty to another, raged at her because the first was not finished and never left her for a minute. She was frantically preparing a meal for the men, and between her rages glanced anxiously out whatever door or window she came near, evidently fearing the men would come before the dinner was ready. Hilda saw that she must bide her time or perhaps spoil her chance of escape. For a few minutes things were so thick in the kitchen that she lost the values of things and the possible destruction of the bridge became a thing of the background rather than the immediate foreground. She hurried around silently, trying to think, setting the table like lightning, her own glances following her mistress's out of the windows and doors as she passed them. The screech of a train roused her thoughts again to her responsibility. What if it were this train that bore the doomed load? What if she had waited too long? She held her breath and listened as an express rushed through. A long line of handsome cars filled with people. She looked from the kitchen window and caught her breath as it reached the bridge. One awful second, it had crossed the first arch! The second! The engine was over on the other side! And now the last car left the bridge and rushed on out of sight among the trees. She turned with a sigh of relief, and caught the eye of the woman full upon her.

"Vat for you stand idle to vatch a drain? You lazy girl! Get you to work. Dem men are coming. Dey vill pe hongry! Dish up the sauerkraut!"

Hilda saw, even as she turned, one of the men creeping up through the bushes, coming up the garden path from the back. They were returning. She drew another sigh of relief! Perhaps she had been wrong. This was not the day for the plot to be carried out. They were only preparing so that they might be ready when their orders came. She would wait until dark and then would steal away. The express train had passed over. All was safe enough. She could be more sure of getting away without being caught if she waited until night. With relief she hurried to put the dishes on the table. The men came in, all but Heinrich, stopping at the pump to wash and joke much as they often did. Hilda tried to stop the ears of her consciousness to their words, for so often their jokes were unspeakably distasteful to her.

The men were jolly, with an appearance of having finished a hard task. At last Heinrich came in and clapped Mrs. Schwarz on the shoulder.

"Well, mother," he said in German, "take a good look at the old bridge. She hasn't many hours to live. We've got her fixed. When the two o'clock freight comes down you'll see her climbing up the golden stairs!"

The other men swarmed in and took their seats noisily, happily, as if some great feat had been accomplished.

Something gripped Hilda's heart like a vise. Her face turned white and her eyes turned wildly to the clock. She was glad the last dish was carried in and she was out in the kitchen where they could not see her. She felt her senses reeling as if she could not trust them. The two o'clock freight! And it was five minutes of one now!

He was on it! *He* was running it! He would not

know! He would come along just as usual, with his dark curly head stuck out of the window, and blow his signals for her. They would echo along the valley with that joyous call that set her heart to thrilling and made her cheeks grow warm, and then the engine would leap out upon the bridge, and — it would *happen! The horrible thing would happen!* It would all be over in a minute, perhaps before the whistle had stopped echoing among the hills. There would be no train, perhaps not even fragments. There would be no more bridge, only ruins! They would find his cap somewhere, miles away! They would never find him! Her one friend would be gone! He would never whistle to her any more! He would be gone! *Germany* had done this! Germany *meant* to do it! *Planned* to do it! Germany did not care for hundreds of lives lost and ruined bridges and unspeakable horrors. Germany deliberately did it! Germany had planned to kill him as if he had been an insect that did not matter! She bowed her head into her trembling hands for a moment and a great shudder passed over her.

And he had saved her life once! Must she, *could* she, let this awful thing happen to him?

She lifted her face with a great resolve. There was strength in her whole body as she threw back her clenched hands and raised her chest. She had been weak, but now she would be strong. She had waited fatally, but it should not be too long! She would do something now! She would fly somewhere and send him word; even if she failed she could rush in front of the train and flag it and tell him the truth. But she must not risk its coming to that. There must be some way to get him word. Would he have left for Platt's Crossing yet? The telephone down in the barn! Could she get him before he left?

She glanced at the clock again. Just ten minutes before his train was due to start. She looked into the dining room. Everybody was eating, laughing and talking, except Schwarz. He was sullen still. He had not found the paper.

She stole to the kitchen door with the broom as if she were about to sweep the porch, and slipping out waited to see if her going had been noticed. Then she slipped quickly down the path to the barn door. If anybody got up to come into the kitchen they would see her straight through the door and down the path. Her feet fairly had wings. When she reached the barn she clutched the door latch and pulled with all her might, but a grim brass lock with a tiny slit of a keyhole seemed to laugh in her face like the Germans she had left behind. She looked fearfully behind her. She heard a chair creak on the bare floor and someone rise and come to the door between the kitchen and dining-room. She could see the shadow of skirts passing the door. In panic she slid around the side of the barn. Then the thought of the precious ten minutes going clutched at her throat. She *must* get into that barn!

6

The end where she was standing was a blank wall with not even a crack through which she might look. She slipped around behind. Oh, joy! There was a short ladder reaching up to a sloping roof, and above the roof was a window. It was high, but perhaps she could reach it from the roof. There was much hay bulging from the window, but surely she could force her way around the hay somehow and get down to that telephone!

With her heart in her throat she began fearfully to climb. She had never been on a ladder before in her life, being a city girl, and at another time she would have felt it an adventure just to try to get up to the roof. But before her eyes as she climbed was the face of the young engineer, and around her there seemed to be his strong arm supporting her for what she had to do.

She gained the roof, but it was blistering hot, and hurt her hands and her knees as she crept breathlessly up, slipping back distressingly every now and then. It was only by shutting her eyes and saying to herself, "I must! I must! The time is going fast!" that she at last gained the wall which held the window, and slowly, cautiously drew herself upstanding on the hot slippery peak of the roof. Could she reach the window ledge? It was high, but she put her slender hands bravely on the sill and struggled wildly in her desperation. There was one awful moment when she thought she was going to slip and fall down the roof again, and then a second when she gained a hold, and, panting, stayed a moment, but at last she struggled to the sill. There was no time to wait and gain her breath and be glad. She must creep through the hay and find a way out. She had dropped inside without thinking that perhaps there was no floor beneath her, but mercifully found it not too far for safety. A few feet from the window she found another ladder leading down into the barn, and she clambered down and stood in the darkness groping about to find the telephone. Her sense of time was gone. She felt as if she had been hours getting here, but she must try at least. She found the instrument by the light of a streak of sunshine that glanced through a crack near the front door of the barn, and clutched at the receiver eagerly, her heart beating so wildly that it seemed as if waves of heat were passing over her and smothering her. It seemed ages before a voice answered her and she could ask for the railroad station at the Junction. More eons passed before another voice responded and she could ask if she might speak to Dan Stevens, engineer on No. 5 Freight, *quick!*

"I don't know as I can get him. It's about time for the freight to move out now, in a minute or two!" came the brusque answer.

"Oh, but you *must!* Something awful is going

to happen on the railroad, and he must know about it before he leaves. Go get him *quick!*"

There was something in the girl's voice that made the man at the Junction rise hastily from his seat at the telephone and shout out the window:

"Say, Tom! Hold that freight! Something's up! Stevens is wanted on the phone! Tell him to hustle!"

Hilda heard and thrilled with hope. A long hot period ensued during which the dusty sweet scent of the hay mingled with her breath while her heart beat so wildly that she could hear it throb in her ears. It seemed as if all the blood in her body had gone into her head. Her senses were so keen that she could hear a distant laugh from Heinrich in the dining-room. Then came Mrs. Schwarz's voice, calling lustily, angrily, from the kitchen door:

"Hilda! Hil-dah! Now vere *iss* that silly girl gone at! Hil-da!"

Hot waves of impatience and fear rolled over her and left her cold and trembling. What if Mr. Schwarz should finish his dinner and come down to the barn before she could give her message? Oh, if she had but told the operator, so that someone would know! For if Schwarz found her here, and suspected what she was doing he might kill her. She had no doubt that he would not hesitate to do so if it suited his purposes. She was so far from thinking of herself that the mere matter of getting killed did not concern her in the least. She was only fearing lest she would have no opportunity to stop the disaster before it was too late. What happened to her seemed a very small matter just then. She was important only because she was the sole possessor of knowledge that was precious to the country and the railroad, and one young engineer whose life was in deadly danger.

What should she do if Schwarz did start to the barn? Wouldn't it be better to drop the telephone and get away so that she could flag the train? Oh, the eternal waiting!

And she could hear the men creaking back their chairs from the table, she was sure. They would be coming in just a minute now! .

Then a clear, cheery voice suddenly spoke in her ear:

"Hello! Stevens at the phone! Who is it?"

Hilda's voice choked in her throat and the tears brimmed into her eyes, but she caught her breath and spoke:

"This is Hilda Lessing, the girl whose life you saved. I've found out they are going to blow up your train today, and the big bridge at Platt's Crossing. You mustn't take your train over the bridge! It's your train they're after because you've got some ammunition on board, they think."

Hilda paused breathless, wondering if she had said all that was necessary, and painfully conscious of the men's voices nearing the kitchen door.

"You don't say so!" came the startled answer of the man over the phone. "Well, I sure am obliged to you for giving me the tip. Are you quite sure? How do you know?"

"Yes, I'm sure. I heard them talk it all out. They don't know I understand German. They'd kill me if they found out I'd told, and I mustn't stay here. But you won't go over that bridge, will you?"

"Not till everything's all safe, little girl, don't you worry! I'll have it investigated. Say, where are you? How can I get to talk to you again? I've got to know more about this. I guess you must have found those spies I told you about."

"Yes," said Hilda in a low, frightened voice, "but I can't stay to talk for I hear them coming. I don't think there is any way you could see me. I never get any time off, and they won't let me mail letters. They read them all."

"H'm! You don't say! Well, I'll find a way to get a letter to you, don't you be afraid. You be looking for it. And you might write me one and have it ready to slip to me on the sly in a hurry. Have it with you all the time. I've got to know about this. You know, if this turns out to be real you have done a big thing for your country. Kid! It's great! I shan't forget."

But Hilda's hand suddenly began to tremble and her heart to fail her. She could hear Schwarz stamping down the kitchen steps. He would be upon her in a moment! She must not be found there! And how could she get out?

"He's coming," she whispered. "Good-bye!" and slipping the receiver softly into place she glided across the dusty floor and sprang up the ladder.

But the ladder was slippery, and her feet and hands were unaccustomed. Schwarz was at the very door, calling back some directions to Heinrich and she was only two-thirds up. She began to tremble and her head swam dizzily. Everything went black before her and for a second she thought she was losing consciousness. Almost her slender hands let go their hold. Then like a whisper of an echo came the words she had scarcely been conscious of hearing as she hung up the receiver. "Take care of yourself, kid! You've been great." Had he said it or had she only imagined it? Somehow the very thought of those ringing kindly words put heart of life into her, and stimulated her failing sense. With new vigor she grasped the rungs and pulled herself up the last long reach, drawing her body safely out of sight behind the hay, just as Schwarz turned the pass-key in the lock and swung open the door.

Hilda gave one glance at the window high above her and knew she would not dare to attempt her freedom until Schwarz had left the building. She wriggled herself softly into the hay, drew her feet back close and held her breath. She wasn't at all sure but a corner of her blue gingham apron was still hanging down in full view, if the man should look up, but she dared not stir again lest the rustle of the hay should arrest his attention. She did not even dare to try and think what she should do next, provided he went out without discovering her presence. It seemed to her that there was nothing possible but to lie here absolutely breathless and wait. Somehow it was enough just now to know that she had accomplished her purpose and saved the man who had once saved her. The penalty would probably fall upon her, and from what she had overheard of the air-man's conversation she judged a penalty from the old country for such a deed as hers would be nothing easy to bear. But she had accomplished her purpose and frustrated their plans. Was that not enough for one lifetime?

Lying in that cramped position Hilda presently became aware that something harder than hay was under and all about her. Sharp hard corners were sticking into her thin shoulders, and her hand was lying against something smooth and cold that struck a chill through her warm flesh.

Down below the man was striding about angrily and muttering to himself in German. A word now and then was intelligible. His cruel face was visible to the girl's glance as he came within her range of vision, and a long slant ray of light fell across his features from a crack in the wall. He was busy about a large box in the far corner of the barn that looked like a tool chest, and presently there arose a queer humming sound. Strange weird prickles went up and down her spine as she listened and wondered. She felt as if everything about her were charged with some unholy death and she in the midst at the mercy of this dreadful man.

Gradually, as she lay there underneath the hay peering out into the dimness of the old barn, things became more and more visible. The rough man seated on a box working away with wires at the tool chest like one playing on a diabolical piano. Now and then a soft blue light flashed up in his face. There were wires reaching from the box to the wall. Her eyes could follow them. They were stretched a few inches apart at regular intervals all over the inside of the barn, even over the ceiling. How very strange! What possible use could they have? Were they telephone wires? But why so many? Hilda could make nothing of it.

Schwarz worked for a few minutes over the box which sputtered and sizzled with blue lights, then he wrote something down carefully, painstakingly, by the light of a pocket flash. Hilda, in her cramped position, wondered if he would stay there all the afternoon and what she should do when the pain in her limbs became unbearable. Suddenly her jailer went over to the telephone and began to talk, calling a number. She wished afterwards she had tried to remember it. Almost immediately he got his man and began to talk in English:

"I ton't findt dot baper! I ton't peleef you leafe it mit me ad all! But I juist gotta message from sea. Dey vill nod land till midnight, so you vill haf blenty time to sent it to me again! Vat? You vill gif it to me now? Sure! I kund wride it down, but you say it vas nod sape? All ride! Go ahead! Rebingdon, Eddystone —"

Hilda's flesh grew cold with horror as she recognized one after another the words written on the paper that lay next her heart! She had a quick flash of realization of what she had done. She was mixed up hopelessly, inextricably, in an infernal machine! It was unthinkable what might her fate not be if she were discovered. She shut her eyes and tried not to think. How many more eternities was that man going to stay down there and keep her a prisoner? And what should she do when he left? Where were the men? Down in the field? How could she get out of the window without being seen by them? She must take her chances. If they were working in sight of the back of the barn there would be nothing for it but to stay where she was until night or perhaps she might risk dropping down the ladder quickly and taking her chances of running away before they could catch her. It was all horrible any way she thought of it. And even if she managed to get out of the barn unseen and back to the kitchen what excuse could she possibly make to Mrs. Schwarz for having been away so long? Where could she say she had been? If she only had some money and could take a train back to some of her friends, they would know how to protect her, but these terrible people would pursue her to the ends of the earth, perhaps, and have their revenge if they caught her!

The minutes lengthened out interminably before Schwarz finally completed his telephoning and went out of the barn, slamming the door shut with a click of the night latch behind him. Hilda waited breathlessly till she heard him go up the path toward the house, cross the piazza and go on down the path toward the station. Then she drew a long breath and pushing the hay back from her face arose to a standing position, trying to get her cramped limbs limbered up for the cautious work they had before them.

A small, thin ray of sunshine slashed through a crack and fell across her feet throwing into relief the spot where she had been lying, and suddenly the girl knew what it was that had been hidden under the hay against which she had been leaning. Guns, they were, dark and sinister, with their ugly barrels pointed right at her, bristling through the hay like an enemy encamped in ambush!

Hilda caught her breath in horror, remembering what she had heard the night visitor say.

94

Then, stooping down, she swept the hay back with a wide, swift gesture and disclosed great stacks of them. They must be stored all over the loft under the hay. She stretched out her hand as far as she could reach, and came against the same hard barriers with only a thin coating of hay over them. There must be hundreds of them! Enough for a regiment! And the man had said they were stored in other places, too! Perhaps the whole country was full of secret places in which were arms ready for an uprising! Perhaps it was true what the papers had been saying, and people had been repeating half in derision, that the Germans really meant to conquer and rule this country — this wonderful, beautiful, free America! How terrible! To have men like Schwarz and the aeroplane man allowed to do with everybody as they pleased. Why, death would be sweet in comparison to a life under such conditions! And all this was really going on and nobody believed it! America was giving freedom and plenty to the Germans within its borders as much as to any other men, and they were abusing the freedom this way! Somebody ought to tell! Somebody *must!* And perhaps nobody knew anything about it but herself. Just one little ignorant frightened girl, who had never been anywhere in the world and knew very little about things. What could she do? How could she explain so that they would believe it, and not laugh the way her teachers in Chicago had laughed at the idea of spies being in this country? She must try and listen and get some evidence to show. Perhaps the paper she had — but how would that tell the Government any more than it told her? She must find a way to get hold of some papers, or letters. The thought was revolting, for her mother had always brought her up to let other people's things alone, but the country was at stake, and was she not a loyal American? She must be a spy herself, if it came to that, and find out what these traitors to their country were doing. To that end, if possible, she must make her way at once back into the Schwarz kitchen and wash those dishes, making the best story for Mrs. Schwarz that she could. She must go at once and work hard and well so that they would approve of her and not suspect her of being a spy against them.

With renewed vigor she turned to the window and put her hands on the ledge to climb out. Then suddenly she heard voices and saw that three of the men were standing in the cabbage patch behind the barn in full view of the window, talking excitedly, and that Schwarz himself, shouting angrily to them, was walking up the path between the cabbages back to the barn. He must have come back by the lower plowed field instead of going to the station.

Trembling with fear, her cold fingers let go their hold on the window ledge, and she dropped instantly into a silent heap of horror back into the hay. Had they seen her? Had Schwarz seen her, and was he perhaps coming back to torture her? She remembered all the awful tales of cruelty and wrong that had been told of the Germans over in Belgium as she crouched in the hay, and listened with senses painfully alert to Schwarz's angry voice, trying to measure how long it would be before he reached the barn.

Then, suddenly, in the midst of her trouble the telephone set up a dull, insistent, violent whirr that almost seemed like a human voice lurking below her, and made her heart stand still with fright!

7

Meantime, while Hilda lay trembling in the hay, several things were happening at the Junction.

Dan Stevens, with his eyes a little brighter than usual — which is saying a great deal, for they were unusually bright, keen eyes — hung up the receiver and handed the phone over to the station agent:

"Call up Dad for me, will you, Sandy, while I get that train dispatcher!" He put his face close to the grated window, laid two of his fingers to his lips and sent forth a whistle that rivaled his signals at Platt's Crossing.

"Oh, I say! Baker! Where's the train dispatcher? Tell him he's got to hold the train till I get this message through!"

Then he swung back to the desk:

"Got Dad? Well, connect me with the other phone then I won't bother you," and he vanished into the little booth at the other side of the room.

"That fellow takes on a great many airs for an engineer, I should say!" remarked a traveler at the ticket window as he received his belated change from the ticket agent. "Perhaps you'd like to call up my grandmother for me?"

The agent eyed the stranger scornfully.

"Nobody has a better right," he remarked with

a withering glance. "His father's the president of the road!" Then he turned with a grim smile and enjoyed the chagrin on the face of the stranger.

Three minutes later the young engineer burst forth from the telephone booth with a smile on his firm lips and a light of battle in his eyes. A word with the train dispatcher, and he swung up into his cab, opened the throttle and set No. 5 booming down the track.

A stubby little man with a face like a purple turnip, and small, curious eyes, watched from his station behind a pile of milk cans and then hurried across the road to a little cigar store where was a telephone. He put his head in at the door and spoke in a cunning whisper:

"You c'n tell 'em *she's went!*" he remarked laconically, and then with an air of having completed an arduous task he lounged over to the saloon and refreshed himself

Three minutes later one of the oldest and most trusted engineers on the road, who had just come in from his regular run and was looking forward to a few hours at his home, received a rush order to take his engine to a certain siding ten miles above the Junction and wait for No. 5.

About the same time, from a city twenty miles beyond Platt's Crossing a group of men, several of them belonging to the Secret Service, tumbled hurriedly on a special train, with every track cleared ahead of them, and sped as fast as steam could carry them toward the bridge that spanned the stream at Platt's crossing

No sound of whistle went ahead to warn of their coming as they approached the bridge. The engine slowing down, came to a halt in the woods. They had their orders not to alarm the people of the region nor to startle any lurkers and put them on their guard.

Silently the little company swarmed from the special and melted into the woods, coming by devious ways through the underbrush, each one in his own appointed spot, to search the bridge and the track in either direction.

When No. 5 reached the lonely siding where the trusted engineer waited, it was the work of but a few minutes to juggle around some empty box cars that stood on the side track, and presently No. 5 thundered complacently on its way to Platt's Crossing, making up time while the most trusted engineer rumbled off on a detour toward the coast with a string of innocent-looking cars racketing behind him and smiling grimly as he thought of home and bed and the rest he would have taken if it had not been for that special order; but he looked back at his train now and then as it followed him round a curve, and there was a complacent triumph in his eye despite the lost rest.

It was just half an hour since she entered the barn, if Hilda had only known it, till the phone rang, and startled her into a frightened heap in the hay again. Then, as she sank down, her senses seemed to come awake.

Schwarz had not locked that door with a key when he went out of the barn! It must have locked itself automatically with a night latch when he closed the door! Why couldn't she then open it from the inside? Why couldn't she get out now, quickly, before he came? There might not be another chance for hours.

She started up, peered cautiously out from the window, saw that Schwarz was still shouting at the men as he backed toward the barn; and then she dived down the ladder, groping her way to the door. There was one heart-throbbing minute when she fumbled for the little knob of the latch, turned it and found that the door yielded; then a glad whiff of fresh air in her face as she held her breath and peered listening through a crack. Outside at last in the blessed sunshine with the click of the softly closed latch in her ears, and the sound of Schwarz's approaching footsteps! She scarcely dared look around, lest she should see someone.

Like the wind, she flew up the path and in the door out of sight, with the thought of Schwarz behind her and the vision of his angry frown before, trying to think what excuse she could give for her absence, and resolving to brazen any questions out by saying she was tired and wanted to get away from the kitchen for a few minutes.

It was like a miracle that she escaped detection. Afterward she used to lie awake at night and live it over again instead of sleeping — that swift rush from the barn to the kitchen! A second more and she would have been caught. Schwarz rounded the comer of the barn and came tramping up the path as she vanished behind the kitchen door and rushed over to the stove to fix up the fire. Always, too, it was a wonder to her that the kitchen had been empty. No one in the dining-room, either! She had expected Mrs. Schwarz to be in a towering rage, but the house seemed unusually silent. Later, when Mrs. Schwarz came downstairs there were heavy dark sags under her small blue eyes, and the end of her nose was swollen and red. Mrs. Schwarz had been weeping opportunely.

Hilda rushed from the kitchen to dining-room with superhuman speed, carrying great piles of plates, knives, forks and cups. There seemed to be special skill granted her to perform the clearing of that table at lightning speed; and all the while her heart was beating furiously at the ominous silence that prevailed in the house.

She glanced at the clock! It was quarter to two. She had been in the barn more than half an hour! At this time of day her dishes ought to have been washed and she at other tasks. To be sure, the mid-day meal had been delayed by the lateness of the men, but she was sure there would be a tremendous tongue-lashing ready for her if Mrs. Schwarz should come downstairs and discover how far behind she was in her work.

She washed away frantically, sometimes just catching a slippery plate or cup from falling in her haste. She heard the barn door close on Schwarz, and heard the faint sound of the buzzer ring again, now that her ears were quickened by her knowledge of the place.

Schwarz came out of the barn twice and gazed off at the bridge with a pair of field glasses, and then went back into the barn.

As the dishes were gradually marshaled into order and Hilda's anxiety about her own position became less, she began to wonder about the young engineer and what he would do? Would they be able to find the powder? Supposing they didn't? Supposing there had been some mistake about it after all and his train had not been threatened? What would he think of her? What would happen to her? Would she be arrested for telling such tales? But there couldn't have been any mistake! She surely had heard it all! And then she went carefully over in her mind all that had happened, even down to the remarks of the men at the dinner table. As the clock hands neared two she began to grow more and more uneasy. What if, after she had hung up, the young man began to think it was all nonsense and decided to run his train over the bridge anyway! What if they wouldn't *let* him stop it! What if — oh, a hundred dreadful possibilities! If she only knew more about railroads and their habits. What was she to presume to stop a great train and save a big bridge!

She gazed off at the beautiful stone arch in the summer sunshine with a gleam of reflection from the water on the gray of its walls, and its feet smothered in living green from the trees and vines that clustered below. It did not seem possible that in a few moments it might be shattered and broken.

And how were they going to find that powder and stop that danger anyway? Would they perhaps come to the house and make the men tell what they had done? And would it be found out that she had told? Well, what if it was, she had saved his life, and she would be glad. Even if she had to suffer afterwards she had saved his life and saved the bridge, and if anybody came perhaps there would be a chance for her to tell about those guns hidden in the hay and about the aeroplane and the barn telephone and the strange night visitors that came to this little quiet farm, and — oh — the message from the sea! What did that mean? There had been a lot of talk about submarines before she left Chicago. Could that have anything to do with submarines? How dreadful that in so fair a world there had to be such awful things to think about! Why couldn't everybody be brave and kind and helpful to everybody else, and not cross and hard and domineering and cruel?

Hilda's thoughts were interrupted by Mrs.

Schwarz's heavy footsteps on the stairs. She hastened to put the dishes away and set the table for supper, expecting a sharp reproof for having been so slow. Instead the woman seemed hardly to notice her. She lumbered over to the door, gazed out down the railroad, then looked at the clock. Hilda wondered if Mrs. Schwarz also was in the secret of the plot, and why had she been crying? Perhaps she did not approve of such terrible things. Perhaps she was afraid of the consequences if they were discovered in their evil plans.

The clock ticked slowly on and it was quarter-past two and then half-past. Schwarz went into the barn a good many times and came out and looked about. The men kept coming up to the house on one pretext or another until at last Schwarz thundered out a rebuke and told them to go to the far lot and plant potatoes. What did they think, sticking around like that? Did they want to arouse suspicions?

Hilda, as she went to and fro in the kitchen, her heart beating so fast she could scarcely breathe naturally, heard and saw it all: watched the great bridge, and the road down to the station.

It came to be half-past two and then quarter to three and still the silence of the hills and valley had not been broken by the sound of a train. Schwarz walked gloomily out of the barn chewing a long straw and looking worried. Heinrich came up to the house for a drink and they stood together a moment outside of the kitchen

"That freight ever been this late?" asked Heinrich in a low tone.

"Ach, yes! Plenty times!" responded Schwarz, but Hilda thought his tone did not sound reassured.

Then suddenly the air was rent with sound, and out from the cut below the station shrilled clear and loud the signal the girl had learned to watch for:

———— ! ———— ! ———— ! ——— ! ——— !

Hilda's heart stood still. She grew white around her lips and things blackened before her eyes. But she must not faint now. She must be strong and ready for whatever came. She must not show by so much as a flutter of an eyelash that she knew aught. Whatever came she must be free from suspicion so that she could get away and tell the Government about those guns and what was threatening.

Outside on the back porch Schwarz and Heinrich stood with suspended breath gazing at one another. Heinrich had the tin dipper half-way to his lips and there he stood, not moving. A gleam of something sinister came into their eyes. Hilda was standing where she could see their profiles without seeming to look. The men were braced as if for a shock.

The train did not stop at the station. It never stopped unless it had freight to take on or off.

Today it ran joyously on toward the bridge. Hilda caught her breath and her hand fluttered to her heart for an instant. Had he then decided to disregard her warning? She listened to the train with fascinated ears, and when it almost reached the first arch she closed her eyes for just a second. Now, if anything was going to happen it would soon be over!

But the train did not seem to slacken its pace. It went steadily, happily on, over the doomed rails; on to the bridge. Each second seemed an interminable time to the girl as she watched it furtively through the kitchen window while she ostensibly prepared the vegetables for supper. The bridge looked so large and safe and permanent. Would it all be gone in another second?

But the train swept on with a happy, almost rollicking sound, arch after arch, over the whole bridge, till its last car dragged itself into the distance and the rumble of its going echoed away into silence. Still stood Schwarz and Heinrich as if petrified, looking at one another with accusing eyes, in which were question and suspicion.

The first break in the tenseness of the moment was by Schwarz in a long stream of profanity and accusation, answered by Heinrich in low, angry rumble, protesting that he had done all as ordered and done it aright! They walked away excitedly to the barn. There was no question any more that she had made a mistake. The two men undoubtedly expected that bridge and train to go to destruction.

Hilda drew a long sigh of relief and the tears came into her eyes. Tears of joy because the young man's life was safe. Relief that nothing had happened after all. But what would happen next?

Mrs. Schwarz hovered anxiously from door to window and back again. She seemed scarcely able to believe her eyes.

Schwarz and Heinrich came out of the barn together. Schwarz was talking violently:

"If I find oud who done id I keel heem, *zo!*" and he brought down his great hoof, grinding the heel into the path with a crunching sound.

Hilda shuddered as she went about her work. She could almost see herself under that heel. Yet she was not sorry she had done what she had.

The air was tense and electric. At times it seemed to Hilda as if she could not breathe. Then she would remember that she had saved the young man's life and a thrill of gladness would lift her out of her horror for a moment. But how had the miracle been performed? Had they found a way in that short time to remove the danger without giving any outward sign? Or had some natural cause intervened to make the peril ineffective? There came no answer to her questions and the hot summer afternoon dragged on. The men were at work in the garden, each one bending to his task as if utterly unconscious that a railroad lay not far away. Yet now and then one or another would lift his head and give a swift, anxious glance at the landscape and then go on with his task. Schwarz went back and forth from garden to house, from house to barn, from barn to the little red brick house, which Hilda, when she thought of it, always called the powder-house. By and by Schwarz had two men bring wheelbarrow loads of bricks and carry them into this little house. They stayed in there a long time as if they were piling them up in a particular way. When they came out they gathered a lot of tools and took them in the little house. Then they locked the door and stood some bean poles up in front of it, as if the door were not often open.

Presently Hilda heard a sound under the window and, glancing out, saw that Heinrich was wheeling loads of earth to the spot directly under her bedroom window and spreading it smoothly over the little iron lid with the ring in its top. He covered it over about six inches deep and then went away and came back with a load of cabbage plants which he set out carefully at equal distances all over the new ground, watering them and taking as much pains as he did with those down in the other garden. One of the other men brought the plow and harrow and some other farm implements and placed them in front of the barn door and later a big reaper was also drawn up in the group, so that it looked as though that door was seldom used.

About four o'clock in the afternoon a hand car

with several workmen came up the track and approached the bridge at a good speed as many another hand car had done in the days since Hilda had come to the truck farm. The car slowed down almost in front of the farm, and the workmen slid off and drove in a few spikes, their great hammers ringing cheerily with a wholesome sound. They stopped three times before they came to the bridge and drove more spikes, and then went on smoothly over the bridge and disappeared. Ten minutes later the afternoon express came down through the opening where the hand car had disappeared, moving at its usual brisk pace, and rumbled pleasantly over the bridge, down the track, past the station and out of sight. Nothing happened! The men relaxed from their energetic farming as soon as its last echo died away and looked at one another questioningly again. There was no question but that they were puzzled. An hour later the up train passed, and still all was well with the bridge.

By the time Hilda had put the supper on the table she was ready to drop with exhaustion and excitement, but she managed to maintain her same dull look when the men came in, even allowing herself to blunder in obeying Mrs. Schwarz's orders, and thereby bringing down upon herself a stream of invectives. The men ate their supper in silence, and with the air of those approaching a supreme moment. They sat down afterward for the evening smoke, but Hilda saw from their glances that they were only waiting for the darkness, to be gone on some important errand.

She hurried through her work and hastened upstairs, gathering her writing materials and sitting on the floor by her window to use the last rays of twilight. She had no time to select her words nicely; the light was fading fast and she had no candle. Indeed, she had learned that it was not desired by the Schwarzes that anybody should have a light in the house at night. They had only one downstairs, and that was early put out. So she wrote, more by the sense of feeling than sight:

Mr. Stevens:

I can't write much because it is getting dark, and I have no candle. They won't let me have time to write by day. Besides, they might find out. This place is full of spies. They have a lot of guns under the hay in the barn, and a telephone, and a queer box with a lot of wires that make a noise and a light. I heard them say there is powder and dynamite here, I think maybe in the little brick tool house. They keep something hid in a hole in the ground with an iron lid over it and a big ring in the lid, just under my window. There are cabbages planted on top of it today, but the earth was just put there. A man comes sometimes in an aeroplane at night and they talk under my window. They say there are going to be uprisings of Germans in this country pretty soon, and they have a list of places that are going to be blown up. The man is educated and speaks both English and German well. This is a terrible place. I have to work very hard, but I don't mind that. I am afraid here. The men are not nice. Will you kindly write my uncle, whose address I give you, to send me money to come back to Chicago? I cannot stay here any longer. They won't let me telegraph, and they read all my letters. Please send my mother word I am well and will write her soon. I am giving her address, too. I am glad nothing happened. I hope you can read this. It is dark, so I must stop.

She scrawled her initials and folded the paper up in a very small square. Then she fumbled around until she found a threaded needle she had used in the morning. She tore a bit out of a worn handkerchief and sewed her letter into a compact little bundle not much more than an inch square, fastened it to a string and put it around her neck, dropping it inside her dress. At least the letter was ready if she ever had a chance to deliver it to the messenger. She had her doubts if even that determined young man could run the gauntlet of all those men and get a chance to see her. But time would tell.

She made a careful toilet and lay down to sleep, fully dressed, determined to be ready for whatever might come. But sleep did not come to her excited brain. Throbbing questions raced through her mind, and she lay trying to plan for a morrow whose nature she could not foretell. Wild plans for getting away contended with wilder ones to remain and find out all that these spies were plotting against her country.

The night was very still outside, and the smell of the fresh earth under her window came up with homely quiet perfume to still her tired senses. The house was very still. Mrs. Schwarz had gone to bed. The men slipped in quietly one by one. After whispering in the dining-room a few minutes they went up to their rooms. Whatever their errand had been they had not remained away long. A heavy gloom seemed to have settled over the house.

Hilda must have fallen asleep at last, for she awoke with a start toward morning to hear voices under her window.

8

For a moment she could not think where she was, so heavy had been her sleep, but then all the day before came back in a flash and she was on the alert at once.

The voices were so low that she could make nothing out. She was not conscious of having heard any aeroplane. She slipped from her bed and stole cautiously across her floor, making slow progress lest the boards should creak. Her eyes were still full of sleep, and she had to rub them to be able to see. There were two dark figures standing below, and the bulging lines of one plainly belonged to Schwarz. He was stooping over, digging at the cabbage plants below her window. He moved one and laid it carefully against the house, pushing away the dirt and disclosing the lid. Silently he lifted it, turned on a pocket flash and the two men descended the ladder. Hilda peered cautiously out the window and watched them. The other man was the man from the air, she was sure, only how had he come? She was sure she would have wakened with the sound of his aeroplane. She heard their cautious footsteps grate along a cement floor and a hollow echo followed them and arose to her ears. After a short time she heard them returning. The visitor was speaking:

"Use the utmost caution! We must not fail again! This has put us back two weeks. It was to have been the signal for the other explosions and burnings. Remember, you occupy a very responsible position. By the way —"

They paused at the foot of the ladder to talk and the words came up as if through a tube.

"Where do you keep that suitcase?"

"Eet iss onder my ped. Eet is berfeckly safe."

"Well, we cannot afford to run any risks with that. I think you had better take it over to Adolph tomorrow. You know that contains a lot of incriminating evidence against us. If that should be found we would all be in trouble. This is no place for it now, with suspicion turning this way. That bridge is guarded night and day, and no one can stir in this neighborhood without being watched for a while. You must not even look in that direction. You must go about your business as if you were nothing but farmers, see? So you had better take that suitcase over to Adolph as soon as possible. There is no telling but they might come and search your house, and it won't do to have it around. You know all the drawings and sketches of the munitions factories are there, and the map with the ports and big railroad bridges marked, besides the wireless code, and those letters from the Prince. If you should be caught with those it would be all up with you! They would search the place and find the wireless, and then everybody concerned would be under suspicion and very likely arrested."

"I petter dake oud the bapers and pud 'em in someding elze. I pud 'em in a pag! Not?"

"On no account! That suitcase was especially made for the purpose. Some of the most important papers are sewed up in its lining. That suitcase must be delivered without fail to the Captain of the submarine next Wednesday. The initials on the end are the sign by which he is to identify it and bear a code message to him. It must be hidden in the weeds by the wireless on the hill overlooking the coast. Your man understands. And have him leave in plenty of time. It is very dangerous for the boat to have to wait around if there is any hitch on our part; he should start a train sooner than last time as delay might be fatal to our plans. Better get that suitcase away from here as soon as possible. Adolph knows all about it, but be sure you give it into *his* hands. We don't want too many in on this. Adolph won't be home till near noon tomorrow. Better take the noon train down; but if I were you I'd come right back on the way-train. You don't want to be long away from here. Bring back a bag of potatoes or something. Now, it is getting light, and I must be going. My automobile is waiting down the road and I don't want to meet any guards. Is there a path across that field to the turnpike? I got out of the way coming over and lost time."

They came up the ladder and the visitor

waited while Schwarz smoothed the earth back over the lid and replaced the cabbage plants. Then they went silently down through the dawning to the garden and disappeared in the darkness. In a few minutes the girl heard the soft purring of an electric car, and Schwarz returned almost immediately afterward.

There was no more sleep for Hilda. Her heart was thumping wildly and she was shivering with excitement. If she could only get that suitcase and put it in the hands of somebody who knew what to do! Schwarz had said it was under his bed! Would she dare slip in there when she came up to make the beds in the morning and get it? Mrs. Schwarz never allowed her in that room. She made the bed herself. But there was always a few minutes in the morning when Mrs. Schwarz was busy in the kitchen and she was upstairs alone making the other beds. She might try. But, oh, what a terrible undertaking for an honest girl who had never laid a finger on other people's property! How like a thief she would feel! And what could she do with it if she got it? The young engineer had suggested the Government at Washington; that meant the President, and how could she get it to him without money?

Schwarz would kill her like a fly if he discovered her. She shivered as she remembered that crushing heel in the cinder path. But what did it matter if she died after all? It was better to die making an attempt to save her country than to live and know she had been a coward and a traitor. Suppose she succeeded in getting away safely, was there any way she could work her way to Washington? Well, perhaps a way would be provided.

Quietly she sat and made her plans, her heart beating like a trip-hammer the while. She would have to go down in the morning just as usual and work. She must not draw attention to herself in any way. She would have to trust to the circumstances to shape her plans when the time came. But one thing she could do now, write a note to Mrs. Schwarz and have it ready to leave where she could read it, so that they would think she had run away to go to her mother and not suspect about the suitcase, nor try to follow her. That would at least give her more time to get away before they discovered the loss. So, in the dawning light of another day she sat on the floor by her window and wrote:

Dear Mrs. Schwarz:

I have got to go and find my Mother. I cannot stay here any longer. I am sorry, but I think you can find somebody who will help you better than I could. I shall find a way to earn my fare to my home, so don't worry about me.

Hilda

Having folded it and written Mrs. Schwarz's name on it, she began to look about on her few belongings with a sinking heart. If she took the

118

stolen suitcase she would have to leave all her own things except what she could wear. It would not be possible to carry more than one suitcase. It would arouse suspicion at once if she were seen. Besides, she must remember that it was going to be a hard trip. She must travel "light."

Softly she went about picking up her few bits of things, folding her garments and laying them in her suitcase. Perhaps some day when the war was over she could send for them. She was glad now that Uncle Otto had not thought it best to let her bring a trunk. He had said she could have that sent later, after she knew what she was going to need. There wasn't much to pack after all. She slipped on an extra skirt and pinned a few little things to the inside of her dress, but she dared not do more lest her appearance be noticed by the family. She locked her suitcase, put her hat and jacket where she could snatch them quickly, tied on her neat brown denim apron and went downstairs to get breakfast. As she started the fire and fried the potatoes and ham she was wondering whether she had better hide her own suitcase, and then it occurred to her that perhaps she might be able to substitute it for the other one. Even if they were not alike it wouldn't be noticed. Her heart pounded away almost to suffocation whenever she thought of the preposterousness of her attempting to steal a suitcase that belonged to the German Government and run away with it; but then a great anger would surge up and a great loyalty to the Land of the Free would uplift her and give her strength again.

Schwarz looked haggard and worn when he came down to breakfast. His unshaven lips trembled when he lifted his cup to drink. He gulped cup after cup of strong coffee, and between times belabored his pitiful old wife with his tongue. When Hilda looked at him she trembled at her own audacity and wondered that she had ever thought of meddling with aught that concerned him.

The men went to their work with an appearance of great zeal, and Schwarz followed them as far as the barn, slipping in behind the reaper and unlocking the door cautiously with many a glance behind.

Hilda went at once to the task of clearing the breakfast table. She was too excited to eat anything, but forced herself to sip a few mouthfuls of coffee lest Mrs. Schwarz should notice.

But Mrs. Schwarz was engrossed in her own sad thoughts. She sat on the side porch peeling apples and taking no more notice of Hilda than if she had been the pump that stood just over the door stone; and Hilda slipped her piece of bread she was trying to eat into her apron pocket and went on washing the dishes.

Suddenly, in the midst of her tense thoughts, she became conscious of a figure standing in front of the door, down by the pump; a barefoot boy with an old felt hat on the back of his head.

He must have appeared around the corner of the house, and Mrs. Schwarz seemed not yet aware of his presence.

Hilda stopped wiping the dish she had in hand to stare at him, but the boy, without an instant's hesitation, lifted a finger to his lips in a swift motion of warning and winked one eye solemnly at her, at the same time putting his hand in his trousers pocket and displaying the corner of a crumpled envelope. Then he pulled off the hat politely toward Mrs. Schwarz and said in a gruff voice:

"Say, lady, may I have a drink of water? I've come a long way and I'm parched to a crisp. I seen your pump and I thought you wouldn't mind ef I come up and got a drink."

Mrs. Schwarz looked up with a start and grunted an unkindly consent, motioning toward the tin cup on the pump.

The boy, nothing loath, went to the pump and brimmed the cup; then sidled back and leaned against the frame of the kitchen doorway, with his back to Hilda, who was still watching him intently.

"Mighty fine view you've got up here," he remarked affably to Mrs. Schwarz, and something white whizzed across the floor behind him and landed at Hilda's feet.

She looked down and saw that it was a letter bearing her name. Breathlessly she stopped and picked it up, slipping it quickly inside her blouse.

121

The boy, meantime, was standing with his back to her in the doorway slowly sipping his cup of water, but his left hand was stuck out behind him, palm open, in an attitude of receptivity.

"You petter pe going!" said Mrs. Schwarz ungraciously. "Schwarz don't like no poys arount. Pe quigk! He iss coming!"

Hilda gave a hasty jerk to the string around her neck, breaking it, and pulling out the tiny sewed-up package. She stepped lightly over to the door, laid it in the boy's hand, and was back at her sink again before Mrs. Schwarz had hardly finished her sentence. The boy's fingers closed quickly over the message, and, dashing his tin cup down, he leaped away over the plowed ground just as Schwarz came around the corner of the barn.

"Who vas dat?" he roared.

"Juist some poy that vanted a trink of vater. I send him apout his pizness."

Schwarz roared something unkindly at her as he came nearer to the house, and Hilda wiped the last dish and fled upstairs to make the beds, every fiber of her being all a-tremble. The letter had really come! She could stop long enough to at least glance it through. It might tell her what to do.

She locked her door and tore open the envelope. It was thick and had several enclosures. If she had but time to read it slowly. But she must take but a second, there was so much at stake.

After all the letter itself was but a few words, evidently written in great haste:

Dear friend:

I haven't but a minute to write before my train leaves, and I won't attempt to thank you for what you have done for me. Besides, it wouldn't be wise. I'll find a way, though, sometime soon. In the meantime I am worried about you. You might need to get away in a hurry if something else turned up, and not be prepared. I am sending you a pass on our road and a little money. Keep them always with you, night and day! If you need a friend, come to my mother. The enclosed card has her address. I have written on the back and she will understand. The bearer will bring any message you have. If you are in trouble, remember the signal. I shall find a way to see you somehow, soon.

Your Friend,
D. S.

Hilda gave one swift glance at the delicate white card bearing the name and address of Mrs. Daniel Stevens. On the reverse side was written: "This is a good friend of mine, Mother; please look out for her. Dan. " The soft color stole into her cheeks as she thoughtfully slipped the card back into the envelope. She looked at the folded green bills wonderingly, and the mysterious little card that was a pass, and slipped them quickly back with the letter, pinning the envelope firmly in a handkerchief inside her dress. Then she opened her door and listened. Schwarz and his wife were having a loud altercation below stairs, punctuated by tears on the woman's part and profanity from the man. Now was the time to get that suitcase if any. Dared she? Somehow she felt strong with that letter in her bosom! And that money! And a pass! How wonderful to have a real pass. Passes were things that only the rich and the great possessed.

Trembling at her own temerity, she stepped across the hall and turned the knob of the Schwarz bedroom cautiously. Then her hope suddenly fell. It was locked! Of course. She ought to have known they would lock it! How foolish she had been to suppose — But stay! There was the key in the door! They had thought it enough to turn it in the lock and leave it for each other's convenience or they had forgotten it!

She turned it slowly, carefully, every nerve tense, holding the knob firmly with her other hand. It grated noisily, but it turned, and the door yielded to her grasp!

9

She peered cautiously in, then ducked low and crept inside on hands and knees, for the opening door had revealed a glimpse through the window of Schwarz's shock head in full view as he stood below outside altercating with his wife.

The bed was smoothed up, and the heavy knitted counterpane hung down to the floor on either side. Hilda pushed the door softly shut behind her and crept across to the bed, lifting up the fringe of the counterpane and peering beneath. There were quite a number of things there: several pasteboard boxes with papers sticking out. A wooden box with a cover nailed down tight, and up against the wall a plain leather suitcase, in size and style much like her own. Breathlessly she reached far down under the bed, straining her ears to be sure Schwarz and his wife were still safely arguing below and would not take her unawares; and finally, by crawling under the bed she managed to lift the suitcase and edge it out on the floor without disturbing any of the other things. Without stopping to look at it she hurried out of the room, and into her own, locking both doors silently behind her. She caught her breath with a quick sigh of relief as she looked down at the stolen article. And now, what? Should she look inside to be sure there was anything of value? She put it on the floor and tried to open it, but it was locked and there was no sign of a key. Schwarz likely carried that in his pocket. She dared not take the time to try to break the lock, even if she had known how. No, she must just trust to what she had heard that this was something containing incriminating papers and let the Government break into it if they thought best. Then her duty would be done. Meantime, this was enough like her own suitcase to be mistaken for it. Why not put hers under the bed in place of the other while there was opportunity? Of course, when they opened it they would have evidence that she was the thief, but she hoped by that time to be far away, and perhaps this would deceive them for a few hours and give her time to get to safety. Anyway, she must take the chance.

She turned it about to slip it against the wall where she usually kept her own, and noticed the letters on the end, C.E.R., painted in black. Seizing her pen and the bottle of ink she turned her own suitcase up on end beside the other and copied them; then quickly slipping the stolen one against the wall by the chair she opened her door, listened a moment, and ventured across the hall again.

It was not so easy to put the heavily packed suitcase back under the Schwarz bed behind all those boxes, and Hilda was panting, dusty and red in the face as she emerged from under the fringe of the counterpane once more and heard to her alarm the heavy footsteps of Mrs. Schwarz coming up the stairs. For a minute it seemed as though her heart would stop beating, and then she rushed wildly to the door and slipped out, closing it, but not taking time to lock it, and slid into the next room just as her mistress arrived at the top, barely escaping being seen. It was a close chance, and she was so upset by it that she could scarcely smooth the sheets as she hurriedly began to make the bed. She was just wondering what she should have done if Mrs. Schwarz had come sooner and found her crawling out from under the bed. Would it have been possible to get out of the window over the porch roof and away? Looking up she saw Mrs. Schwarz with an angry face standing in the door! It startled her so that she jumped and dropped the pillow she was puffing up.

"You pad, lazy gute-for-nodding girl!" scolded the mistress. "You haf nod made one ped! I cannot trust you oud of my side a minude! What haf you ben doing?"

With quick presence of mind Hilda drew out her handkerchief and put it to her eyes:

"Mrs. Schwarz, I am troubled all the time that I do not get a letter from my mother! It seems as if I could not stand it!"

"Ach! Himmel! Is dat all? You vill haf worze drubbles pefore you get a liddle older. You haf pin a paby. Now you haf to pe a voman! You get downstairs and pud on dem wegetables! Aftervords you get dem peds done qvick! You hear?"

The woman turned and went into her own room, but the sound of the closing door was suddenly drowned in the distant rumble of the eleven o'clock train coming on through the cut beyond the station. Hilda, knowing that her time had come if ever, sped to her own room, grabbed the stolen suitcase, with her hat and coat, and rushed down the stairs.

The note she had written to Mrs. Schwarz was in her coat pocket. She fumbled wildly for it, paused an instant to be sure Schwarz was not in the dining room, and flinging the note on the dining-room table hurried to the door. One frightened glance showed Schwarz vanishing down the path toward the cabbages with a hoe over his shoulder, and the other men hard at work in the distance with their backs to the house. The train almost reached the station. Could she catch it?

She was off, speeding with the fleetness of a wild thing over the plowed ground, panting and clinging to the suitcase, over the roughest place in the field because it was a short cut.

Then, suddenly, out from the upper window, came a hoarse, angry scream! Mrs. Schwarz had discovered her flight, and now all the forces of hell would be put in motion to bring her back!

With breath coming short and eyes that tried to locate and register the doings of the train, and could not because everything swam before her in a kind of black mist, Hilda quickened her pace. She caught her toe in an ugly root and fell headlong across a furrow, striking her knees against a stony spot and grinding her chin into the earth. Dazed and sick with fear she clung to the suitcase, but her hat went whirling away several feet down a little knoll to the side, and she had no time to go out of the way for it. In imagination she could already see the men with Schwarz at their head, pursuing her, and the train moving off without her. If she did not get that train she had no refuge. They would catch her, for they were men, and powerful; and she was almost at the limit of her strength already. What were hats in such an emergency?

She sped on wildly, dragging her coat by its sleeve, and struggling blindly over furrow after furrow, the blood in her head, her breath coming painfully, her senses so stunned by the fall as to be unable to tell whether or not the train had started. Now and then a shrill cry, or a rough call reached her ears, and she knew that she was being pursued, but on she went till she reached the last little knoll above the station, where the train was in full view. She could see now that the wheels were beginning to turn and the train was moving slowly out. Her lips were moving in a gasping prayer: "Oh, God — make them stop!

Save me! Save me! Save me!"

The passengers at the windows had an exciting moment as they gazed at the flying girl with streaming hair, wildly waving a little dark jacket in one hand and gripping to a suitcase with the other. She was coming on at a tremendous pace, while behind her came a file of four big men in working clothes, all running as hard as they could go, and wildly waving hoes and rakes and shovels in a threatening manner. It looked like a violent attempt to hold the train till the girl reached it.

But the conductor was cross that morning. He was already ten minutes behind him and had to make up besides, he did not like Schwarz; so he gave no signal to stop and the train moved on.

"That's a nervy little girl!" exclaimed the passenger in the seat near the conductor. "She hasn't slackened her pace one iota. I believe she thinks you'll stop for her yet."

"Well, she'll find herself mistaken!" growled the conductor as he ducked his long neck to watch her from the window.

"I believe she intends to jump the train!" said another passenger, rising in his excitement. "See! She's coming right at it, and she has that look in her face."

"No!" said the conductor angrily. "She couldn't do that! She'd have too much sense. Those Dutchmen have got to learn a lesson. They're always bothering me with something.

Sometimes it's a letter they want mailed special, sometimes it's some market stuff they haven't got ready. They are always trying to hold me up a minute or two late! I won't stop for anybody today!"

"She's going to jump!" said the excited passenger. "Look at her!"

The conductor gave a low horrified exclamation and reached for the bell-cord. The passengers rose in their seats with one accord, and a wave of horror and admiration went through the train.

On came Hilda, her second wind coming to her now, and her head growing cooler with her danger. There was no turning back for her. She had gone too far. She must make that train or die under its wheels. She had an innate sense that such a death would be far preferable to what she would meet if she failed and fell into the hands of the Germans.

She was but a car's length from the platform now, but the train was under good headway and going faster all the time. She looked with calculating eye, coming straight on with bounds like a young deer, and marking well the rear platform of the next to the last car. One more spring, a step or two alongside and she had caught the hand-rail with one hand and swung to the lower step, the suitcase in the other hand flung ahead up to the platform. What a mercy the conductor had been too busy watching her to put down the platform over the steps and make it impossible for her!

The dark blue jacket which had been hanging in her left hand slipped away when she took hold of the rail, quivered for an instant against the car and then shivered down under the rails and lay a crumpled, dusty ruin where the girl would have lain if she had missed her footing; but Hilda huddled on the lower step, clinging still to her suitcase and the hand-rail, panting and dazed from the shock of alighting.

The train was slowing down and the conductor had opened the car door. The girl lifted her head, saw the men still running toward the train frantically waving their farm implements and realized that her danger was not yet passed. She must hold out a little longer before relaxing. Rallying her senses she scrambled to her feet, the conductor helping her, and scolding her soundly in terms she did not even hear, so anxious was she to show him she was all right and he might go on his way. She was too far spent to speak, but she smiled bravely up into his face, utterly unnerving him, and stopping the flow of invectives he was heaping upon her unconscious head. He looked at her hard, thought how her sweet little flower face would have looked beneath the cruel wheels, brushed his big hand across his eyes and reached for the bell cord, giving it a mighty pull. The whistle sounded, the wheels turned again and the train started on its interrupted course.

Nobody had noticed the stampede of oncoming men, and Schwarz was almost to the station, puffing like a porpoise and swearing as only Schwarz could swear when he really tried. When the passengers had assured themselves that the girl was safe, they turned for a belated vision of the men and saw Schwarz shaking an angry fist in the distance, and the other three men still wildly waving, respectively, a hoe, a rake and a pitchfork. They afforded an interesting moving-picture for a brief moment and then the train with Hilda passed quickly out of harm's way and they were forgotten.

Hilda, still puffing and panting, but smiling bravely, dropped into the little end seat at the back of the car, utterly unaware of the interest she was exciting among the passengers, who stood up, craned their necks, and spoke their commendation of her feat in no hushed tones. She was only aware of the conductor's cross, kind eyes upon her, and his gently gruff tones when he tried once more to tell her that she must never do such a thing again, that she might have been killed. She wanted to tell him that she wouldn't, no never, as long as she lived if she could help it; that she was fully as frightened as he at what she had done; but her breath wouldn't let her, and so she only smiled; and he, still scolding, made his way up the aisle taking tickets.

It was some time before he came back to her

and Hilda had quite recovered her breath and her self possession, although she was still trembling all over. She had become aware of the interest she was exciting and it made her uncomfortable. She looked down at herself. No wonder they stared. She was still wearing her brown denim apron, and she had no hat nor coat nor gloves! It was her first realization that her hat and coat were gone. The little purse, with its dollar and a few cents in change, too, was gone with the coat, tucked safely into the pocket! The little purse that her mother had given her at parting! It is strange how at a time like that the loss of a small thing that is dear will stand out with a sharp pain.

She set about making herself tidy. She could see in the glass of the window that her hair was rumpled, and she smoothed the braids and bound them trimly about her well-shaped head again. She leaned down and rubbed the thick mud from her shoes with a newspaper someone had left on the floor. She set the suitcase well inside the seat, changing around the end that bore the lettering so no one could see it, and spread her scant gingham skirts protectively over it. Then she looked down at her apron and decided to remove it. She rolled it up neatly, pinning the ends of the belt about the bundle, and realized that she had done all that was possible toward bettering her appearance. The reflection of her bare head in the window glass troubled her. If she only had a hat! It looked so queer to go traveling bareheaded. Of course, some people did have their hats off now, but when she reached her destination how noticeable she would be! She looked wistfully down the aisle at a girl with a long black braid of hair hanging down her back and a little red and black swagger cap tilted on one side of her head. That was a simple little hat. If she only had something she could make one in a few minutes, but she was without a thing that could help! Nothing but a strange, locked suitcase, supposedly filled with dreadful papers, and an old brown denim kitchen apron rolled up and fastened with two pins! She couldn't very well make a hat out of an apron and two pins. Stay! Couldn't she? How was it she used to fold bits of kindergarten papers and make paper caps for her brother when he was little? Could she remember the trick of it? Why couldn't she fold her apron up somehow and pin it to form a cap? It was the same color as those brown trench caps the soldiers were wearing. It would be much better than nothing, and perhaps nobody would notice her very much. She would try, at least.

She unrolled the apron and began her task, folding it this way and that, experimenting a little, and presently, sure enough, she had a little brown denim cocked hat, the point of which she folded over to one side and slipped under a fold, pinning it firmly. She tucked the apron strings smoothly inside, folding them precisely and pinning them with the other pin. It wasn't a wonderful hat, of course, but it would pass for a hat at a glance, and it was really quite becoming to her pretty face when she ventured to fit it on her head. The kindly window glass reflected back a stylish contour as she surveyed it fearfully, deciding that it was certainly better than nothing.

The conductor was coming back, and Hilda hastened to fumble in her blouse and bring out her precious pass. As she handed it out she was beginning to be conscious again of her strange position, and to fear that everyone would suspect her. It was new to her to have anything to hide, and it troubled her deeply.

The conductor looked at the pass and then flashed a curious, surprised, deferential glance at her. His tone was respectful when he addressed her:

"Feeling all right, miss? That was a narrow chance you took. Sorry I didn't see you sooner!"

Then he made his way back to the other end of the car and stood with puzzled eyes on her and a speculative brow, his chin in his hand. When the brakeman came through he confided in him:

"Mighty queer for a girl like that to get on at that station. I never saw her around there before, did you? She doesn't look like the rest of that crew. She's traveling on a pass!"

The brakeman started.

"A pass!" he cast a quick, apprising glance

down the car again.

"H'm! That's queer!" His voice had a shade of disappointment. He had thought he might just stop and ask if she felt shaken up by her scare or anything. He had noticed her pretty face and graceful movements and was nothing loath to have a word with her, but brakemen didn't make a practice of conversing with persons who traveled on passes. He braced himself against the door and folded his arms meditatively, his eyes on the outline of a brown denim trench cap.

"What do you reckon she is, a servant of one of the big men on the road?" he asked presently.

"She doesn't talk like a servant, nor look like one," answered the conductor, getting out his tin box and beginning to sort out his tickets.

"She might be a governess or something."

"But what would she be doing at that German dump? She doesn't look like one of those."

"Search me," said the brakeman with a shrug.

Nevertheless, he hovered near Hilda's seat all the way to Philadelphia and was most assiduous about opening and shutting windows when they went through a tunnel, eyeing her appreciatively whenever he passed through the car, which was often.

10

Hilda was utterly unconscious of the admiration she aroused. She sat quietly looking out the window mile after mile, seeing little and thinking much. She was fully awake and alive to possibilities now. She realized what she had done, and in what danger she was. She had thought to get off the train at its next stop, but the train hadn't stopped yet, except at a forlorn little shanty much like the station at Platt's Crossing. If she got off there she would only have to take another train to get away from there, for there wasn't a vehicle or trolley in sight, and she couldn't walk far across country with a heavy suitcase. Besides, time was valuable. If her information was valuable to the Government, it certainly was necessary to get it into their hands as soon as possible. She sat with unseeing eyes upon the passing landscape, trying to make herself realize that she was a thief running away from the law, but somehow she could not make it seem real. All the same, being a city-bred girl and knowing the swift ways of modern justice, she knew that Schwarz would probably pursue her with every means at his command, especially if he discovered the loss of his precious suitcase before her own passed out of his keeping. Her only hope was that the note she had left would throw him off her trail and make him think she had gone to Chicago. It was entirely possible, of course, that in his haste he should not notice the difference in the suitcase. However, she must take no chances now that were avoidable. She must not be caught and dragged back to the farm, or, worse still, put in jail, before she was able to tell what she knew to the President or someone in authority.

She canvassed the possibility of confiding in the conductor and putting herself under his protection until she should reach Washington, but after studying his face a little while she decided against it. He was kind, but he might not know how to hold his tongue, and it was better to keep her knowledge to herself until she could tell the right person. If only Dan Stevens were engineer on this train, how easy everything would be! She could send him a note and he would give orders to have her looked after until she was safe. But he was not engineer, and she decided it was best not to take too many into her counsel.

She had no idea where she was going, beyond a vague notion that the train was moving east. The precious pass had protected her from any questions as to her destination. If Schwarz should telegraph to the conductor of the train he would be bound, perhaps, to give her up. It was just as well he should know nothing. She must plan to evade him somehow.

The train was stopping often now at small villages, and she began to wonder if she ought to get off and strike across the country to another railroad or in search of a trolley. Then the fear of delay caused her to sit still a little longer. She could see more houses in the distance, a lot of them, and smokestacks; perhaps they were nearing a city. It would be so much easier to hide in a big city! If she only knew where she was! The names at the little stations along the way told her nothing as to her whereabouts, because they were all little unknown places not on the map. But this seemed like a big town, with rows of roofs, and red brick walls, and houses huddled in rank and file. Should she get out? She would wait till the name of the place appeared, and perhaps that would help her. Just then the attentive brakeman flung open the door near her and sang out: "West Philadelphia! All out for West Philadelphia! Next stop Broad Street Station!"

Hilda settled back in her seat again. Here was something to go on. She knew where Philadelphia was, of course. It was down at the southeastern corner of Pennsylvania, one of the big cities of the United States. In her mind she could see it on the map now, and Washington was only a few inches below it. She was on the right track. But West Philadelphia would likely be a small station on the outskirts of the city somewhere. She would go into the big station and perhaps buy a hat and coat before going to Washington. It would be dreadful to go to see the President looking as she did!

She sat quietly watching the people about her, those outside on the platform standing in the murk and gloom of the tunnel, the people crowding in and looking in vain for empty seats. She almost forgot to fear that a policeman might be in the crowd, till she sighted a big man with brass buttons just outside her window. He was not looking at her, but she shrank back with frightened heart and was glad when the brakeman slammed the platform down and shut the doors, and the train moved on again, out of the tunnel into a great city, between high buildings, towers and domes. A thrill passed through her at the thought that she was seeing another big strange city. What a thing to tell her mother when all this dreadful business was over and she was free to go and search for her! Then her thoughts were suddenly jerked back to the present as the man in the seat ahead of her leaned over and stopped the passing conductor.

"Are we much behind time?" he asked anxiously. He held his watch in one hand and an open timetable in the other.

"Only ten minutes now," responded the conductor. "We lost forty minutes, but we made up thirty."

"What chance do I stand catching the Washington Express?"

"You ought to have got off at West Philadelphia!" scolded the conductor, as if the man was to blame for not knowing better.

The passenger sprang to his feet and looked back as if he might repair the wrong: "I've got to make that train to Washington!" he cried.

"Too late now," said the conductor, pushing him back in his seat. "Sit still. I guess you stand a pretty good chance of making it if we don't get halted on the track before we get in. She lays on the next track just across from where we usually come in. She's mostly there every day when we get there, pulls out just a minute or two after. You just be ready the minute we stop and hustle across the platform. Yes, over on this side. You can't miss it. It's only a step. You'll see the Pullman cars. Don't wait to go up to the station. Just beat it right across."

The man thanked him and got his belongings together, anxiously watching out the window for the first sign of pulling into the station.

Hilda's resolve was taken. She would follow that man to the Washington train. She would be all ready to move the instant the train stopped. And the man wouldn't know it; nor would the conductor. She would just slip out as if she knew the way perfectly well. She had her pass, and in case it shouldn't happen to be good on the Washington train, she had money enough in that big roll, surely to carry her to Washington. She needn't wait for a ticket. She could pay on the train.

The man bustled his hand luggage back to the door to be ready the minute the train stopped.

The conductor came along, lifted the platform, opened the door, and the man stepped down to the lower step as the train slowed into the big car shed at Broad Street Station. Hilda watched furtively, but would not move till the train came to a halt, and then she was at the steps as the man swung off. He started to run up the platform to where a train was just puffing up preparatory to starting. She tripped down the steps lightly, dodged behind a baggage truck and was off after the man.

"Is this the Washington train?" she heard the man ask as the conductor leaned down from the platform, his hand up to the signal cord.

The conductor nodded, the man sprang aboard, and Hilda after him just as the wheels began to move. She had to catch at the hand-rail to keep from falling back. The conductor had gone in the car without seeing her. As she followed the man into the car she caught a glimpse of the attentive brakeman gazing anxiously down the platform with a disappointed expression, but she did not know that he was looking for her. Up at the station gates a stout man with a red face and blonde hair was studying each passenger who came through with keen, anxious gaze, and a German woman with a little shawl around her shoulders questioned the conductor as he came up to the gate about a girl who had got on at Platt's Crossing with a suitcase. The conductor told her the girl had been on the train. The brakeman asserted that he was sure of that; she better look in the waiting room. He tried to get the woman's address but failed. He wouldn't have minded going to see if Hilda got to her people all right, he thought. One didn't see a girl like that every day. She was apparently far superior to her people. Likely she was city-bred and had been out to the farm to visit relatives.

Back at the West Philadelphia station another man in citizen's clothing watched the trains awhile and then went into a telephone booth to report his failure at Platt's Crossing and get more particular directions. Meantime, Hilda sat in the little end seat of the Washington train and sped on her way without hindrance, thankful that so far no one had molested her.

The afternoon dragged on and the car was hot and crowded. A large woman in a satin gown sat down on the end of Hilda's seat and crowded her close against the wall. There was no window by that little end seat, and the place was dark and close. It was many hours since the voices under her window, before daylight, had roused her to the world, and she had come a long, hard way. Her lashes drooped over her pale cheeks, her head and her back ached terribly, and she felt a great goneness in the region of her stomach. She had eaten no breakfast, and the few mouthfuls of coffee she had taken had long ago lost their effect. She longed to lie down and cry, she was so miserable and hot and faint, but she dared not even put her head back and close her eyes lest she should fall asleep, because of the precious suitcase which she must guard every instant. There must be no rest for her until she put the burden of responsibility into the right hands.

A colored man in a white linen coat with a pad and pencil in his hand passed through the car and drawled: "Last call for dinner in the dining-car," and she longed to follow him and get something to eat. She had money, why should she not? Then a swift glance at the large satin person beside her dozing ponderously, decided her against it. She would have a time struggling over those great satin knees, and maybe her suitcase would be seen, and she would be brought into the notice of those about her. If Schwarz had sent word to the police, there was no telling but someone was around watching her. It would be better to sit right still and wait. There wasn't the least likelihood of her starving in one day and she certainly had nerve enough to sit up and bear a little discomfort for the good of her country. It wouldn't be half as bad as going to war, and having to live in wet, muddy trenches; eat anything you could get; fight, and get wounded; or die alone.

She drew a little sigh and straightened up, trying to fix her attention on the people around her and keep herself awake. It seemed hours she had been on that train. How far was Washington? Would they never get there? The man

145

she had followed into the train had faded away into a parlor car. He was doubtless even now regaling himself with a good dinner. Well, she would play she was sitting opposite to him ordering what she liked and he was telling her all about the sights along the way. Wouldn't it be nice if she had people to go with her to places, and talk to her, and laugh with her! Ah! Well, she would play it again, and maybe some day it would come true.

She thought of the young engineer. What if he had been the man and had taken her into the diner and ordered roast beef and ice-cream! Ah! Her head reeled at the thought of the food, and she sat up very straight and called herself to order. She simply must not faint or get sick or anything to attract attention. She wondered what the engineer would think when he found she was gone. But, of course, he wouldn't find out now until she got somewhere and wrote him or telephoned to him. She had left the little red scarf hanging out of the window. It had been her last act in the morning before she went down to get breakfast. Had he seen it today when his train went by and would he try to find out what it meant? She had hung it there because the thought had come to her that perhaps in some terrible way she might be shut up or made away with before she could get the knowledge of the spies to the proper authorities, and she had a vague feeling that if Dan Stevens knew there was something to be alarmed about he would ferret it out in some way.

The three hours passed at last, and just as the sinking sun was sending long, opalescent lights into the sky, a city dawned on the windows of one side of the car, with a great white shaft rising like an angel out of the sky, and a big white dome a little farther on. There was something about the sight that reminded Hilda of the pictures of the Heavenly City in Pilgrim's Progress, and she caught her breath and sat up very straight. This was Washington. She knew without being told. She had seen pictures, and, anyway, if she hadn't she felt she would have known. It was different from any other place she had ever seen.

She followed the passengers from the train, her head feeling light and dazed as if she were in a dream. At a desk labeled "Information" and draped in flags in the center of the wonderful marble station, Hilda asked the way to the White House, and was told to take a certain car out in front of the station.

There were long rosy lights over the city as she emerged from the station portal and stood waiting for the car. There in front of her, only a seeming stone's throw from where she stood, was the great Capitol Building that had graced the outside of her geography, and been framed in photograph and hung in her schoolroom, and which had seemed almost as wonderful and unreal to her all her life as heaven itself.

Everything seemed white and green to her wondering eyes. Great white buildings, hotels and houses, other buildings of enormous size for which she had no name, white palaces set in living emerald. How wonderful to have this glimpse of it all! For a moment she forgot the strain of her tired arm that held the heavy suitcase, and stood gazing with delight. Then came the car and she got in and was whirled on down into the city, through more wonders.

She had asked the conductor to let her off at the White House, and it seemed but a very few minutes before he touched her arm and pointed kindly which way she was to go. She got out of the car, walked a few steps, and at last arrived before a great iron gate behind which stood a man in uniform, with two or three soldiers in the background pacing up and down. She put out a timid hand to find the latch, but a gruff voice informed her that no visitors were admitted to the White House now! *The country was at war!*

Hilda's hand flew to her heart in alarm, and she stood still ready to cry. To have come so far on so important an errand, and not to be admitted! What should she do? But she had not come all this way to give up so easily! She lifted her white face to the big officer.

"Why, I know there's war," she said timidly. "It's that I came about. I have some very important information, and I must see the President

148

right away. I've come a long distance just on purpose."

"Well, you can't get in here without a permit! You'll have to go away and get a permit! There's hundreds of people every day trumping up excuses to see the President, and I can't let anybody in."

Great tears came unbidden into Hilda's eyes and she suddenly sagged down on the suitcase and dropped her face in her hands.

"Oh, what shall I do?" she cried, feeling that she could not stand up another minute.

"Say, look here, lady," said the officer peering over the grating with concern. "Don't carry on like that! Why can't you be reasonable? Don't you see I've got my orders?"

But Hilda sat still, her slender shoulders shaking with the sobs that, much to her chagrin, had mastered her for the moment. She was nervously unstrung. But it was only for a moment. She brushed away the tears and lifted a very determined little face to the man at the gate.

"I'm sorry to act so silly," she said, "but I've been traveling since early this morning, and I haven't had anything to eat. I've simply *got* to see the President somehow; I suppose there's a way if I only knew how. Couldn't you tell me, please? This is very important. It's about some spies, something I've found out that ought to be known at once. Really, there isn't any time for delay! They are planning some terrible things!"

The officer looked perplexed but shook his head.

Suddenly a voice just behind her startled Hilda.

"What's all this? What's the matter here?"

Hilda looked up and saw a tall man in an officer's uniform of olive drab. The man at the gate saluted him promptly and explained:

"Only a young person, Captain, who says she has some information about spies, for the President," he laughed half apologetically. "There's been hundreds here today, and they all had some good excuse to see the President."

The soldier eyed the girl sharply as she rose and stood before him eagerly repeating her plea, the weariness and tears all gone for the moment, and only a sense of her mission upon her now.

"There might be something to it, you know," said the soldier, turning to the officer at the gate. "Where did you say you came from?"

"I'd rather not tell anything about it until I find the President. I don't know you, you know," she added naïvely, "and I don't think I ought to tell anybody but him. Couldn't you show me how to find him?"

"Well, how do you know but I'm the President?" asked the soldier with a smile of amusement.

Hilda looked up keenly, and a quick color came into her face. She knew he was ridiculing her, but there was a kindly twinkle in his eye.

"Why I've seen his picture," she answered smiling. "I'm sure I should know him. You're not the President. Please take me to him."

"Well, I can't take you to him, for it wouldn't be possible just now, but I can take you to someone who will hear what you have to say and will tell the President all about it if it is anything he needs to know. Come this way!" and the gate swung open at his motion, the blue-coated officer standing aside and saluting with an "All right, Captain! Just as you say, Captain!" and Hilda walked on beside him. He reached out to take the suitcase, but she shook her head.

"Thank you, no. I'd rather carry it myself," she said with a faint smile, and he smiled indulgently back at her. Somehow there was something about Hilda that made him think her story might be true. And yet there were *so many* people with all sorts of ruses!

Hilda found herself, presently, seated in a great leather chair beside a grave gray-haired man in uniform, who was writing at a desk. He paid no attention to her for some time, going on with his writing, and issuing orders now and then to men in uniform who came and went. There was something about him that convinced her that he was a good man and would know what to tell her to do even if he was not the President. Anyway, she was in Washington, and the White House was close at hand. She wasn't sure whether she was actually in it or only in an outer building in the same grounds, but it was really the White House, for it was just like the one in the pictures. And if they were so very particular about keeping people out of the grounds on account of the war, they surely wouldn't have a man about the place to whom it would be unsafe to tell everything. The sense of relief and of having at last reached a place where she could unburden her terrible secret and get rid of the responsibility made her feel dizzy. All at once the big white room with its white ceiling and many leather chairs began to whirl around curiously and get in the way of her seeing the man. She gave a little gasp and relaxed against the back of the chair. The gray-haired soldier turned suddenly and caught her as she fell.

11

When Hilda came back to consciousness she was
lying on the other side of the room among leather
pillows on a deep leather couch and someone was
holding a glass of something to her lips. A big
electric fan was moving over her and the kindly
gray-haired soldier was standing near and asking
if she felt better.

Hilda was much ashamed that she had shown
her weakness and tried to sit up, protesting that
she was all right now, but her white face and
trembling body belied her words. The officer
told her to stay where she was for a while and
asked if there was anything he could get for her,
or did she wish him to send for her friends. Then
Hilda fully came to her senses and sat up in spite
of his protests, looking wildly about for her suitcase. What if someone had stolen it from her
while she was unconscious! But it was over by
the desk safe and sound where she had been sitting, and an orderly, at a word from his chief,
brought it to her.

"Thank you" said Hilda, much relieved and
resting her head back again. "It isn't my own,
that's why I'm so worried, and I think it's very
important. I brought it for the President to see.
Could you please send word to him that I am
here? Tell him I came a long distance to tell him

something terrible that some spies are going to do very soon. I heard them talking about it under my window. I had to start away very early and I've had no chance to eat anything. It was a long time and very hot, and I guess that is why I felt dizzy. I'm sure I never fainted before."

The soldier explained to her that the President was away from the Executive Mansion for several hours, and that in any case it would be impossible for her to see him until her mission was fully known.

"I am the one who would have charge of this matter. It comes under the Secret Service," he said kindly, and drawing back his coat showed her his gleaming badge.

Hilda drew a sigh of relief. She remembered that the young engineer had mentioned Secret Service. Why had she not thought of it before?

"You can tell me whatever you would tell the President," said the officer. "But first you should have something to eat."

He gave an order for a tray to be brought.

"Perhaps, however, you would prefer to have me send for your friends, and let you get a good night's rest? Then you can come and see me in the morning if you really have something important to tell," he said pleasantly.

Hilda sat up promptly with a flush in her white cheeks. She had not come all this way to get a good night's rest.

"I have no friends," she said quietly, "and

morning might be too late. Mr. Schwarz might find me by that time and kill me, so I couldn't tell you. He is a terrible man!" She shuddered at the remembrance of his face when she had suddenly appeared in the barn the day before.

"He is working for the German Government and he doesn't care what he does," she went on. "They are planning to have a big German uprising just as soon as there is a victory in France. They have guns and rifles stored in a great many places, and they are plotting to blow up a lot of munition plants and shipyards and factories. They almost blew up a bridge yesterday just to wreck a trainload of munitions, and they'll do it again as soon as they get a chance. There isn't a minute to lose. Something has got to be done about it."

Her eyes were shining and she was talking excitedly. The other men in the room stopped talking to listen; and at a motion from their chief, came over and sat down nearby. They all looked at her keenly. At last they were willing to listen!

"How do you know this man is working for the German Government?" asked the chief.

"Because a man that came in an aeroplane at night several times stood under my window and talked about it, giving him orders. He said 'The Fatherland is depending on you,' just in those words. And he told him all about the uprising, and what he was to do. He talked very freely, because they thought I didn't understand German."

The chief suddenly touched a bell for his secretary and drew up his chair ready for business.

"Will you please begin at the beginning and tell everything," he said. "Who are you, where do you come from, and how did you happen to be near this man Schwarz?"

So Hilda sat up and began to tell her story to an interested audience.

Meanwhile, back at Platt's Crossing, several things had been happening.

As the train swept away from the station bearing Hilda and her precious suitcase, Schwarz stood helpless with rage and bellowed invectives of the vilest kind after her. He swore at the men and ordered them to do so many unreasonable things that they got out of his way entirely, lest he might in his wrath do them some personal injury.

Schwarz raged up to the house and began roaring at his wife for having let the girl out of her sight. The poor woman protested in vain that it had not been her fault, and finally discovered and produced Hilda's note, which did somewhat to assuage the underlying fears in Schwarz's heart, lest Hilda had seen and heard more at the farm than would be wise to have reported to the world at large. He sat down weakly at last in the dining room chair and took the note in his two trembling hands, relieved to be assured that the girl had gone to her mother.

"Weak, silly fool!" he muttered, and then began afresh with a new set of horrible adjectives for Hilda and his wife and the whole of womankind in general, in which after a few turns he included Uncle Otto Lessing for having landed such a good-for-nothing upon him.

Suddenly the dining-room clock cleared its throat with a preparatory whirr and began to strike the noon hour, and simultaneously there arose a distant roar of an oncoming train.

Schwarz started to his feet livid with anger again and turned upon his long-suffering wife:

"Dat drain! I must it dake! Dat sood-gase unter de ped! Ged him quig!"

Like a mad man he stormed up the stairs with his fat, weeping wife puffing behind and getting in his way. He swept boxes and other impediments out of his way, pulled forth the suitcase without a glance at it, and stamped down the stairs again, pushing Mrs. Schwarz aside as if she had been another box.

The train was roaring distinctly now, just crossing the bridge, and Schwarz waited not for hat or coat, but all as he was in his shirt-sleeves with his yellow-gray hair bristling in the breeze, went lumbering over the plowed ground to the station, carrying Hilda's suitcase. A little way behind him wallowed Mrs. Schwarz, faithful to the last, tears running down her flabby cheeks, her under lip still quivering from the fray, and in her hand Schwarz's best coat and hat. She took the hardest, shortest way across the plowed ground and made slow progress, arriving too late to be of service, and Schwarz took his hatless way to "Adolph's" in no wise improved in temper by the state of his attire.

Three-quarters of an hour later the express slowed down at Platt's Crossing and let out two passengers, a slender little wisp of a woman in black and a small boy. The train took scant leave of them and hurried on its way. The two strangers stood bewildered and looked about them.

They cast one glance up at Schwarz's house, deserted now as the men were in at dinner, and then turned away. That was not at all the place of their expectation.

"I thought your uncle said it was right by the station," said the woman, "but I don't see any place around here that could possibly be it. He said it was a very large, handsome place. Let us walk back down the track a little way. We passed two nice-looking farm houses. It must be one of those. It is strange there isn't anybody around to ask."

The boy looked alertly down the track.

"It's a long way back, Mother. You stay here and I'll run up to that little house on the hill and ask."

The mother looked up at the hill house again and shook her head.

"Oh, I don't think I would. There might be bulldogs up there, Karl, and I should be frightened to death if they came after you. No; we'll walk back this way. I'm sure there was a village back there and we can hire a carriage and drive to the right place. It won't cost much in the country, and that will be much better than hunting around everywhere and asking people who don't know anything."

Karl gave a lingering look at the house on the hill, put his two fingers in his mouth and brought forth a long, peculiar whistle.

"There! If Hilda's around she'll hear that and come to the door!" he said as he turned reluctantly to follow his mother down the track.

"But Hilda wouldn't be in a house like that, dear," said the mother smiling. "Your uncle said it was a very nice place."

"You can't most always be sure about Uncle Otto," said the boy shrewdly. "Look at that asylum! Good night! He thought *that* was good enough for *you!*"

"I really don't believe your Uncle Otto knew how bad things were there, dear. I'm sure he didn't."

"Then why didn't you tell him and have him getcha a better place?"

"Well, dear, I thought it was best not to trouble him any more. He is a busy man, and I thought we would just come down and see how Hilda was fixed, and then find a nice place near her. We'll get a couple of rooms for the present, and I can do sewing and embroidery, and by and by we will save up and all be together again."

"Well, all right. Only I'm going to get a place to work on the farm and begin to earn, too, right away! Remember that! I'm no baby any more. I'm nine years old, and it's time I was taking care of you!"

The mother smiled indulgently, and they walked on down the track tugging a big valise between them.

Karl's whistle had brought the men in Schwarz's house instantly to their feet, with Heinrich at their head, and they peered cautiously out the open door, with Mrs. Schwarz's tear-stained face looking out the open window, but when they saw nothing but a woman and a child they melted back into the dusk of the room again, all but Heinrich, who stood on the porch watching them thoughtfully.

The mother and boy turned back once and saw him standing there.

"There! See! I'm glad you didn't go up to that house. I don't like the look of that rough man. Let's hurry away!" said the mother.

They walked for nearly half an hour without apparently getting any nearer to the little white village that hung like a mirage in a distant valley; then they reached a field of young corn where a laborer was hoeing quite near to the fence and inquired the way.

They turned reluctantly back again, drooping wearily on the side that carried the valise, the boy tugging to get the whole weight away from his mother, and she in turn lifting her side higher than need be so the weight would not fall upon the boy.

"It must have been further on in the other direction," said the mother with a troubled look at the long blinding track beaten upon by the high sun.

"I'll bet it was that ugly little house on the hill," said Karl. "I'll bet it was just some more of Uncle Otto's big talk!"

"Hush dear! We musn't judge before we know! Maybe we'll find her in a lovely big white farm house with green blinds and a stone walk and hedges, and white hens walking around the thick grass on yellow kid feet. That's what I've always dreamed of a farm house being. And a cow that gives cream, and a row of bright milk pans, and bright little garden close to the carriage drive."

"S'pose you don't! S'pose it's *that* house where she is?" asked the child after a long pause.

"Then I shall certainly take her away with me at once," said the mother with spirit. "I couldn't think of leaving her in a place with a lot of men like that! We'll manage somehow. Hilda and I can get work. And you know I've got fifty dollars yet after buying our tickets. I didn't tell your uncle I had that. It seemed almost like deceiving him not to, but I thought if anything happened I'd like to be able to get to your sister at once without asking anybody for a loan. I worried a little bit about not turning that over to your uncle when he told us your father owed him so much, but you know really that was my own money. I earned it myself at embroidery. It wasn't your father's money. You don't think that was dishonest, do you, dear? I wouldn't like to do a thing that seemed that way to you, even if you are young, because you might think later when you grew up that it gave you an excuse for not being always perfectly honest."

"No, Mother! I think you were perfectly right. I don't think Uncle Otto had any business with our money, anyway. I don't believe Father owed him all that! I believe he's a — he's a — well, Mother, anyhow I *hate* him! I do! I just *hate* him for letting you and me go to that horrid old 'sylum and sending Hilda off alone when she wanted to teach!"

He stopped short on the track and, setting down the bag, mopped his hot young forehead defiantly.

"There, there, dear! We better not talk about him any more. It isn't right. And besides we don't *know*. We just think, and that's wicked to think evil of people. Let's talk about the day. Isn't it beautiful off on that hill? See those clouds."

162

"It's hot!" said the boy, "and you're tired. Gee! When I get to that farm house where you say Hilda is, I'm going to lie down in that thick green grass and let the hens walk over me with their yellow kid gloves while you go in and find her. I'm hot and sleepy."

They walked on back to Platt's Crossing and then more slowly on down the track, looking ahead.

"There aren't any houses over there at all, Mother! It's just woods and a bridge!" declared the boy, after they had traveled anxiously for another five minutes. "We'll just *have* to go up to that house and ask. You couldn't ever walk over that railroad bridge; it would make you dizzy."

"Well, we'll go together then," said the mother with determination.

Once more they turned back and this time climbed the path up to the Schwarz house.

12

Mrs. Schwarz sat gloomily on the porch paring potatoes and heaving deep sighs of despair. She did not see her visitors until they were almost upon her.

"Can you tell me where Mr. Schwarz lives?" asked a clear voice in German, and she looked up startled.

She surveyed her visitors stolidly, but finally admitted that Mr. Schwarz was not at home.

"Oh! Then he lives here!" The visitor caught her breath sorrowfully and looked at the boy with a faint smile of apology.

"I have come to see my daughter, Hilda," she said to Mrs. Schwarz. "I am Mrs. Lessing. Will you be kind enough to tell her we are here?"

But Mrs. Schwarz did not move. A great wave of dark red swept up over her swarthy countenance and her under lip came out ugly:

"Your taughter iss not here!" she hissed. "I know nodding apout her!"

"Oh, then perhaps there is another Mr. Schwarz near here! Could you direct us?"

Up the track beyond the station rumbled the two o'clock freight, not stopping at the station, but rattling noisily by; and opposite the house came the clear, piercing whistle, three long blasts and two short ones. But for once Mrs.

Schwarz did not look toward the train at the signal. She rose from her chair, letting fall her pan of potatoes with a clatter, and came toward her visitor angrily:

"No, there iss no other Mr. Schwarz, and I know nodding apout your daughter. Get you gone! Ve do nod like gumpany! My man vill be home soon und he vill nod haf beeble around! Your daughter Hilda vat you call her iss nod here!"

She was speaking in broken English, perhaps to stop her visitor from talking German, and she looked wildly toward the garden where the men were working. She did not notice that the little boy had slipped away around the house. His mother stepped back courteously from the porch:

"Oh, but I have not come to stay with you. I am not company. I shall make you no trouble. I merely wish to speak with my daughter a moment," she said in English with a quiet dignity that checked Mrs. Schwarz for a moment.

"I dell you she iss nod here! Your daughter iss nod here!" reiterated the overwrought woman.

The freight train a rod or two from the bridge had come to a sudden halt. Train hands with red flags ran out ahead and behind, and the engineer leaped out of the cab and slid down the cinder parapet to the fence, which he vaulted easily and came striding up through the furrows of plowed ground, making short work of the trip. But neither Mrs. Schwarz nor her visitor noticed. Down behind the powder house Heinrich, carefully hidden in the bushes, with a pair of field glasses, studied the train.

It happened that the engineer's route of travel was hidden by a row of elderberry bushes in full leaf and bloom. Heinrich was worried about those flagmen, but he did not see the engineer.

The engineer made straight for the house, approaching it from the side where Hilda's window looked. He came flying along with his eyes on a little red signal fluttering languidly from the window, and he was so intent upon it that he almost fell over a small boy who stood under the window also looking at the red signal.

"Hullo!" said the engineer, catching himself just in time. "What are you doing here?"

The boy looked up loftily:

"I'm looking for my sister. The woman out there on the porch says she isn't here, but I know she is, for there's her scarf up there in the window. I know it, for it used to be mine. I guess I couldn't make a mistake about a scarf I hated and used to wear to school and the fellahs all made fun of, could I?"

"Well, I rather guess not," said the engineer heartily. "Say, young chap, what's her name?"

"Hilda Lessing," said the boy, eyeing him suspiciously.

"Well, I'm looking for your sister, too, and it's that very scarf that brought me. She agreed if anything went wrong with her to hang out a red signal and when I saw that I thought she might be in trouble. You're sure that's hers, are you?"

"Sure!" said the boy scornfully.

"Well, then, here goes. Have you called her?"

The boy nodded disconsolately.

"And she didn't answer. Well, suppose you shin up on my shoulder and get in at that window and see if there is anything else of hers up there in that room. If there is, we'll find out where she is or we'll know the reason why."

The boy gave the stranger's clear brown eyes one searching look, sprang into his arms and scrambled up to his shoulders. Slowly, carefully, he was lifted up till his fingers grasped the windowsill and he could pull himself up and look in.

"Nope!" he said disconsolately, shaking his head. "Nothing! Aw, wait! Here's a handkerchief. Yes, that's Hilda's. It's got her name written on the corner in Mother's writing."

"Reach in and get it, old man, and get a hustle on; someone might be coming, and we'd rather catch them than have them catch us."

The boy struggled a moment and reached a handkerchief down on the floor by the window where Hilda had dropped it. Then slowly he was lowered till he sprang to the ground. A strange, hollow sound reverberated under his feet as he dropped, and he looked down doubtfully, stamping at something hard under the earth.

"Gee! That sounded funny!" he said.

"It certainly did," said the engineer, looking thoughtfully up to the window and down to the ground again. Then he drew out a crumpled sheet of paper and glanced over some writing on it. He put the paper back in his pocket, and, stooping down, began to dig in the soft earth with his hands.

"We'll investigate this matter," he said cheerfully, "but don't make any noise. I have an idea."

Carefully he lifted out two cabbage plants and laid them to one side, then scooped away the earth and revealed a big iron ring.

"Just as I thought!" he remarked. Then looking up, "Say, son, just cast your eye about and see if anyone is watching. Give me the high sign if you see anybody."

The boy looked cautiously around and the digging went on rapidly. A moment more and the engineer lifted up the iron cover and peered down the ladder into the hole.

"Just one second more, son," he said softly. "You're on guard. I'm going down. If anyone comes, whistle!"

He disappeared down the hole and Karl stood by, his eyes large with wonder. He stood his guard faithfully, looking in every direction, almost holding his breath in his earnestness. In a moment more the young man was back again, springing up the ladder and putting the iron lid back into place with set jaw and a light of battle in his eye.

"Just help me camouflage this up, won't you, son? We've got to cover our tracks and then beat it. No, your sister isn't down there. I guess she's all right. Anyhow, we're going to find her. Just hand me that off-cabbage, will you? Smooth that side up. Don't leave any footprints. Now, we're ready. Take your scarf around to Mother and see what she says."

Mrs. Lessing was standing in the path a little way from the house, a look of mingled distress and dignity upon her gentle face when Karl shot around the corner of the house waving the scarf.

"Mother, she's here all right, somewhere. See what I found in her window!" he shouted.

Mrs. Lessing grasped the scarf and looked up frightened.

"It is my daughter's scarf!"

Then, seeing the engineer, she appealed to him.

"Sir, I wonder if you could help me to find my daughter. She is staying with some people named Schwarz on a farm at Platt's Crossing, and this woman says she is not here."

The young man flashed a courteous smile at the woman, noting with satisfaction that she looked as much of a lady as did her sweet young daughter, and then turned to Mrs. Schwarz, large and red and towering on her porch.

"You are Mrs. Schwarz, aren't you?" he hazarded.

169

Mrs. Schwarz did not answer.

"Well, Mrs. Schwarz," went on the young man commandingly, "you will have to tell us at once where Miss Hilda Lessing is or you will find yourself in serious trouble. We have found her scarf and a handkerchief with her name on it, and it is of no use whatever for you to deny that she is here. Will you call her at once, or shall I send for the sheriff and have you arrested?"

Mrs. Schwarz grew suddenly white and reeled toward her chair with a clutching hand outstretched to the back.

"It iss the truth!" she cried broken. "She iss nod here! She has runned away! She vas a pad girl und vould nod stay!"

"You can't expect us to believe that, Mrs. Schwarz!"

"But it iss the truth! She runned avay this early morning and shumped on de drain ven it vas already started. She leaf a letter on de table! She haf gone to her mudder!"

"Where is the note?" demanded the young man.

Mrs. Schwarz, with a fearful glance toward the garden to see if any of the men were watching, tottered toward the door and presently came out with the letter.

"Tague id und go pefore my husband cumes bag!" she implored. "He iss very ankry. He vill haf kill me for it showing to you."

The young man glanced through the paper

and turned to Hilda's mother:

"Mrs. Lessing, is that your daughter's writing?"

Mrs. Lessing took the letter with trembling fingers, while Karl eagerly peered over his mother's shoulder:

"Sure! That's Hilda's writing!" declared the boy before his mother could collect her shaken senses to read it.

"Yes! It is Hilda's," she declared a moment later. "Oh, where do you suppose she has gone? She didn't have any money. Unless, perhaps, you paid her; did you, Mrs. Schwarz?"

"Ach! No! I never haf money und Schwarz say she vas nod vorth id."

"Well, take this, Mrs. Schwarz, and don't say anything about our visit to your husband. Then he can't make you any trouble. We're going away now, and he needn't know we have been here," said the young engineer, putting his hand in his pocket and handing out some money.

She gazed at the ten dollar note he had given her in utter amazement and then eyed him suspiciously. That was a big sum of money for an engineer to hand out recklessly all at once like that. But money seldom came her way and she grappled it to her with a swift, ingathering movement and absorbed it in her ample bosom, murmuring:

"Ach! Vell!"

Then, with a frightened glance about to see if

171

she were being watched by the men, she toppled into the house and shut the door.

The young man turned with a half laugh and a shrug to the distressed mother:

"Mrs. Lessing, I think it would be wise for us to beat it! Will you accept the hospitality of a freight train to the city, or would you prefer to wait at the station for a passenger coach? I'm afraid you might have quite a wait for the afternoon and that station isn't very comfortable. Besides, I can't keep my train waiting any longer and I would like to talk to you. I know your daughter just a little and I will do my best to help you find her."

"You are very kind," murmured the bewildered woman. "I don't want to put you to any trouble, but I don't know what to do. If Hilda has gone back home, perhaps I ought to follow her to Chicago."

"H'm! That's an idea! I must find out which train she took and we can easily trace her and catch her by wire. Son, you take your mother down across the field to the freight train you see. Go just as straight and as quick as you can, and I'll be with you in three jerks of a lamb's tail. Understand?"

Karl nodded like a soldier taking orders from a beloved officer and taking his mother in tow with a firm young hand piloted her over the field toward the fence while the young man strode across the porch and sought information of the vanished Mrs. Schwarz. A moment more and he was skimming over the field himself in long bounds, reaching the fence in time to help the lady over, and fairly carrying her up the bank to the train. She hesitated and gave a troubled look at the long line of freight cars.

"I'm sorry it isn't any better," he said dubiously, "but it's the best I can do for accommodations at present, and we really ought to hurry to the next station where we can wire your daughter as soon as possible. It seems she got on the train going east, and she likely will land in Philadelphia. I think we can catch the train by wire at West Philly. I'm behind time, but I'll try to make up if you don't mind sitting on a box in an empty car for a few minutes. I'll just swing you up and then I'll get ahead to my engine as quick as I can. After a bit I'll get a chance to come back and tell you about things."

Heinrich, watching behind his powder house, saw the train begin to move again and drew a long sigh of relief. Thanks to the thick growth of elderberry, he had not seen the strange passengers nor the maneuvers of the engineer. After the train had crossed the bridge and vanished out of sight, he went to the house and hunted up Mrs. Schwarz.

"Did you see what was the matter with that freight train stopping?" he asked her.

"No, I been to zleep!" she responded with a grouchy yawn, and Heinrich departed to hunt up the other men.

The freight train rumbled its way to the next station and its unexpected passengers sat on two boxes and looked at one another.

"It's all very strange," said Mrs. Lessing. "How do I know that this young man is all right? How do I know where he is taking us? And what does he know of Hilda? Perhaps he is in league with these people. I cannot understand what your Uncle Otto could mean. There must be some mistake."

The tears blurred into her pretty, tired eyes.

"Don't you worry, Mother! That engineer's all right. He had a letter in his pocket from our Hilda. I saw it when we were out back of the house. He said he was worried about her himself. Trust me, Mother. I know a man when I see him."

Karl was sitting up very straight with importance and excitement, holding the little red scarf clasped tightly between his hands, and looking out eagerly on the passing landscape. To think that he should get to ride in a freight train like this! It was unbelievable delight! Perhaps, when the young man came back he would take him up and show him the engine, or maybe let him ride in it with him. His very finger tips tingled with the daring thought.

The mother smiled through her tears.

"Yes, dear, but you might be mistaken. And how in the world would a young man, an engineer, have a letter from Hilda? Why, she doesn't know any young men, and she wouldn't even talk to a stranger — our Hilda! She knows better. No, dear, I'm afraid something is wrong. I believe we had better get off when this train stops again and just slip away. We can telegraph Uncle Otto and ask him what to do."

"Not on your life, Mother! Don't you do that! Uncle Otto would be mad as a hatter that we left his old asylum. Just you stick by this guy for a while and see. He knows what he's about and you can't tell but Hilda has met him, all right. Anyway, what's being strange when he's nice? Why, he's simply great, Mother! He lifted me right up on his shoulders to the second-story window, so I could get this scarf and Hilda's handkerchief. And, say, Mother, there's something awful queer about that place! There was a big hole in the ground with an iron lid, under the plants, and we dug up some plants and looked in. I guess he thought maybe they had Hilda hid down there. He went down into a kind of cellar with a ladder, but she wasn't there, of course, and then he covered it all up and put the plants back again. He looked kind of funny when he came up and he told me to be real still. I mean to ask him what he saw down there when he comes again. Maybe there was some bombs down there. Maybe that Mrs. Schwarz is a German spy!"

"Nonsense, child! What queer notions you do

get. Your father always said that was a news-paper lie. He said there were no German spies."

"Well, maybe he didn't know," suggested the son shyly.

The mother cast an anxious glance ahead. She was scarcely listening. The long train rumbled itself up to a station and stopped. The freight car where the two passengers sat was high and dry above a steep embankment. Mrs. Lessing stood poised in the open doorway studying the distance to the ground and trying to make up her mind to get out when the young engineer came flying up to the door.

"Now, Mrs. Lessing," he said cheerfully. "I've wired Philly, and I've found out that that train will be in Broad Street Station in half an hour. I've given directions to have the conductor at the phone when I pull into my next stop, so I can talk to him. Then we'll know what we are about. Meantime, I hope you haven't been too uncom-fortable. I've sent one of the men back to the ca-boose for some cushions, and I've got my rain-coat up here in the engine to spread over it. I think we can make you a more comfortable place than that box to rest. You can lie down if you like. And then if you'll let the kid come up in the cab with me I'll show him a thing or two about engines. My name is Stevens, Dan Stevens, and I met your daughter down at the Junction by ac-cident the day she arrived. I had the honor of pulling her away from before an express train, and naturally we found out each other's names. The other day she returned the service by telephoning me just in the nick of time about a plot she had found out to blow up a bridge and wreck my train, so you see we're rather well acquainted, although we've never seen each other but once."

"Oh!" gasped the mother. "How perfectly dreadful! And now she's gone! And no telling what other terrible thing has happened to her!"

"Don't worry, Mrs. Lessing. She has a level head, and she'll turn out all right. We'll soon be on the track of her. I suspect she had to run away from those people. There's pretty good evidence that they are German spies!"

"Spies! Oh, no! How dreadful! How could that be? My brother-in-law said they were good friends of his!"

"Well, I suspect a good many of us are liable to discover that we don't know all about our friends in these days. But, anyway, don't worry, Mrs. Lessing. Here come the cushions. You just lie down a bit, and I'll take the kid up front with me."

At the next stop it was discovered through telephone conversation with the Philadelphia conductor that a young girl had boarded the train at Platt's Crossing, but had disappeared at West Philadelphia, and no one seemed to know when she got off. The young man rushed back to reassure the mother that her daughter was probably safe and sound in Philadelphia; and to tell her that he had just been talking to his own father in that city, who had promised to use all possible means to locate Hilda at once.

Mrs. Lessing shed a few quiet tears as the train went on its lumbering way once more, but her growing confidence in the young engineer enabled her to be on the whole quite calm, and when her son came scrambling back to her at another stop with a glowing account of his wonderful ride on the engine she began to take a more cheerful view of things. After all, if Hilda were in Philadelphia, it would be a good place for them all to stay and begin a new life together.

Arrived in Philadelphia at last, the young man came for them, neatly dressed now, without his overalls and greasy cap, and looking like any handsome young man.

He had a studied air of cheerfulness about him, but one who knew him well would have read the little pucker between his eyes as betokening anxiety. He escorted Mrs. Lessing into the station to freshen up her toilet after the rough journey, and betook himself to the telephone booth. Ten minutes later he met her once more in the waiting room, still with that studied air of cheerfulness.

"We haven't got on the right track yet," he said, "but I think we will soon. Father has wired all the trains going toward Chicago that left West Philadelphia after she reached there, but she does not appear to be on board any of them. However, that is nothing. She may have thought best to stop overnight and rest; or wire you in the west before starting. If you will give me your former address that may help some. Also I would like a description of what she would probably wear, although as she may have left in a hurry, that might not be a guide. You don't happen to have her photograph, do you? Good! That will help! And, by the way, our road detective is on Schwarz's track. Before midnight he will know just where he has been this afternoon and whether he was trying to trace her and bring her back. You see she did some rather important detective work for the road and her country yesterday, and if Schwarz suspects that he may try to catch her and hide her; but we shall soon find him out, so there is nothing to worry about. Now, Mrs. Lessing, unless you have friends in Philadelphia with whom you prefer to stay, I would be very glad to have you come home with me. My mother will, I know, make you welcome, and doubly so when she knows that your daughter saved my life yesterday."

And so, amid the poor woman's protests and hesitations, and the eager pleading of the boy to go, young Daniel Stevens, Jr., led his guests away to a taxi and they were soon on their way to his father's house.

13

When Hilda had finished telling her story the men plied her with questions. Did she see a wireless anywhere about? What did the inside of that barn look like? What sort of wires had she spoken of as being stretched on the barn walls and how were they arranged? Just how did the man look who came in an aeroplane and how many times did he come?

When she described him the men nodded to one another.

"I guess it's the same chap. He must be in charge of the whole ring in this part of the country."

In the midst of it all the orderly entered with a great silver tray on which were all manner of good things to eat, beginning with soup and fried chicken and ending with ice-cream and coffee. The tray was arranged on a little table and the men had the courtesy to withdraw to the other end of the room and consult while Hilda ate her supper.

Such a good supper! Delicacies that she had seldom seen, and plenty of everything. Even the war bread was delicious, and from her long fasting tasted doubly so. Right in the middle of it, before she had even tasted the ice-cream, she remembered the suitcase, and jumping up, she ran over with it to the chief.

"I forgot all about this!" she said eagerly, "and it's perhaps the most important thing of all." She set the suitcase down in their midst and told the story of how she stole it and got away on the train with it.

"Well, you certainly are some nervy little girl," said one of the officers, as he watched her sensitive face light up with her story. "Now, what do you expect to find in that suitcase?"

The chief reached over to take it.

"If it contains all the evidence the night visitor suggested it will be the biggest find we've had in this war, Miss Lessing," he said with his courteous smile.

So Hilda stood by, forgetful of her melting cream, while they broke the lock and examined the contents carefully.

There was little inside that told her anything. Papers with writing and drawings, of whose importance she could only judge by the look on the faces of the officers and their low exclamations as they passed the papers from one to the other.

She slipped back to her dinner after a little and watched them from afar as they read, examined and commented in low tones. She saw that they were disappointed about something. Had they not after all found what they wanted? Suddenly she remembered. The lining! Some of the important papers were sewed up in the lining!

She slipped over to the men again.

"Won't you please look inside the lining?" she said timidly. "That man said some of the most important things were there. He said the suitcase was especially made for the purpose, and that it must be delivered to the captain of the submarine by next Wednesday night. Those were his words."

The chief picked up the empty suitcase again and they all clustered about him and began to examine it. Carefully they cut away the lining and disclosed some more very thin papers. Gravely the chief examined them and passed them to the others with a knowing look and then sat back and looked at Hilda:

"My dear young lady," he said earnestly, "I have the honor to inform you that you have performed one of the greatest possible services for your country. These papers give the key to our enemies' plans and will enable us to frustrate them. Without these we might have gone on for months helplessly in the dark. You need have no fear; your information shall certainly be placed in the hands of the President, and I have no doubt he will see you himself and let you know what he thinks of your bravery and patriotism. Your promptness has saved many lives and much property, and may be a key to the ending of this terrible war. And now, I know you must be weary after your long, exciting day, but there are just two or three questions I would like to ask before you go."

Hilda's heart began to sink. Where was she to go? But then, she had money. She could go to a hotel. She would ask this courteous soldier where was a safe place. She gave her attention to his questions.

"Will you tell me once more about your telephoning to the Junction? To whom did you telephone? Daniel Stevens, an engineer? A friend of yours? I see. He had saved your life and you wanted to return the favor. Do you know where this Daniel Stevens lives and what his route is? I wonder if we could reach him by phone tonight? I suppose the railroad department can look that up for us. Better do it at once. Now, what was it? Daniel Stevens, No. 5 Freight —"

"Excuse me, Captain," spoke up one of the officers. "That couldn't by any possibility be D. K. Stevens's son, could it? You know he is doing practical work on the road preparatory to going to France in charge of a company."

"Oh, not likely," said the chief.

But Hilda was fumbling in her pocket and bringing out a letter from which she extracted a small visiting card.

"This is his mother's address," she said quietly. "He wrote this note to me and sent it by a little boy with some money and a pass. He said if I ever needed a friend I was to go to his mother, but I think that's in Philadelphia. Perhaps you ought to read the letter," and she surrendered her precious letter to the astonished gaze of an interested public.

One of the officers picked up the white card.

"Well, that's who it is!" he exclaimed. "Dan Stevens! You better get him on the phone, Captain!"

"Yes. Get him on the phone at once!" said the Captain, looking up with startled eyes. "Don't waste a minute. If he isn't there, perhaps his father is. I want to talk to him. This puts a new phase on the whole matter! D. K. Stevens's son!"

Hilda settled back in her chair again, a sudden weariness and faintness coming over her. Something in the tone of the men and the way they spoke of this Dan Stevens made her feel infinitely removed from him. After all, her work was done, and it was time now for her to drop out of things and find a spot in the world for herself — this big, weary world that somehow didn't need her!

She put her head back against the chair and closed her eyes while the men were talking. She knew that the secretary had gone to the telephone in the little booth behind the desk and that presently they would somehow be in touch with the young engineer. Then her responsibility would be at an end. Probably she would never see him again. It gave her heart a heavy tug to realize that. Well, never mind! He was not of her world, anyway. He had been kind, and made her life a little more bearable during those awful days at the truck farm and she could remember him that way, and keep his letter to help out the pleasant memory — that is, if they gave her letter back. They might need it for evidence. Well, he had saved her life and she had been able to save his, and so they were even! Now she must set about getting into communication with her mother!

She opened her eyes suddenly and realized that the Chief was standing by her chair and addressing her:

"My dear young lady, I am afraid that in the excitement of the occasion we have been most neglectful of you. You are very weary, of course. You must go at once to your rest. Have you any —"

But Hilda interrupted him gravely:

"I was just going to ask you if there was any plain, cheap place not far away where I could stay tonight? In the morning I must start back and try to and my mother."

"Why, certainly, certainly; we'll find a suitable place for you. And it may be that we shall have to ask you to stay here several days. We may need you for evidence, you know. This is a very important matter, affecting the country's best interests. We must keep in touch with you until everything is perfectly plain. Meantime, I shall find a comfortable place for you to stay and a suitable companion. You will be the guest of the Government, of course. You do not need to worry about the price. But excuse me just a moment. They have my number on the phone!"

Hilda sat back again too bewildered to think, half frightened at the prospect. She had never dreamed that her duty would detain her longer than to tell her story. The tears were brimming near the surface, and for one awful moment a lump in her throat threatened to overwhelm her, but she conquered it as she sat white-lipped and tried to get control of herself. Of course, if she was needed she must stay, and perhaps it was right they should pay her necessary expenses as long as they needed her. Meantime, of course, she could telegraph to her mother, and find out what she ought to do. But how could she stay in a great city without more suitable clothing? She looked down at herself in her little brown working gingham, and her hand went instinctively up to the improvised hat, which, all unknown to her, looked very sweet and pretty on her shapely crown of hair, with its little rumpled waves and curls slipping loose about her tired face. To the young men who watched her furtively she seemed a pleasant picture.

There was, however, deep distress in her eyes when the Chief hurried back a few minutes later, and she began to speak at once.

"Excuse me," she said, "you have been very kind, but I don't believe I can stay any longer than tomorrow morning. Couldn't I tell you all that is necessary now and then go? You see, I haven't anything with me. I had to run away just as I was, in my working clothes, and I dropped my hat and coat on the way to the train and couldn't stop to pick them up because Mr. Schwarz was almost up to me. I had to pin my apron together into a hat to wear on the train."

She touched her brown denim hat with a laughing apology. The eyes of the officers went to the innocent looking cap in astonishment. There was nothing to suggest an apron in that shapely little crown. It seemed to them that any pretty woman might have worn it to advantage.

"You see, I couldn't bring any of my own things along because I had at the last minute to leave my suitcase in place of the other one, so they wouldn't discover theirs was gone. Mr. Schwarz was to take it to 'Adolph,' whoever he is, on the noon train, and I suppose he may have taken mine; so I'm not likely to get hold of my own things again if he carried out his program and gives it to the captain of the submarine on Wednesday night."

"Why, what's that? You don't say!" said the Chief sitting down again. "I forgot all about that submarine business and 'Adolph.' You say they have your suitcase? Well, that's interesting. That gives us another clue. I wonder if you could tell me just what was in that case?"

There ensued another conference in which

Hilda gave a complete list of what was in her own suitcase, and told in detail once more the story of the bridge plot and how she put a stop to it. This time she told about the paper on the ground containing the list of names and how she had got possession of it by means of toothpaste and her ink bottle. Her audience was so much interested in the story and her cleverness, and above all in the little paper which she produced, that they congratulated her again and again upon what she had done. She almost forgot her weariness, and her perplexity about where she was to spend the night, until suddenly the Chief remembered and exclaimed: "Here we are keeping you at business again when you ought to have been resting long ago. By the way, Mr. Stevens just told me that he has been trying all evening to trace you. His son phoned about your disappearance. It seems you hung a signal in your window before you left, did you?"

The color flamed into Hilda's white cheeks.

"Yes," she nodded. "I hung out my little red scarf. He told me to put something red in the window if I got into any trouble."

"Well, Dan Stevens saw it and went to investigate. They traced you to West Philadelphia, but lost track there."

Hilda's eyes shone. To think that he had seen her signal and stopped his train! It was too wonderful! How kind and good he must be! Of course, that was not surprising now that she had discovered he belonged to a great family — and yet, wasn't it even more surprising when one thought it out? That a man of consequence should stop to think of a little working girl in whom, of course, he could have no interest save a passing one?

The telephone bell interrupted her thoughts, for the secretary who answered it came out of the booth immediately saying:

"Mr. Daniel Stevens, Jr., wishes to speak to Miss Lessing."

Hilda grew suddenly cold and hot all over to hear the formal announcement. It seemed to put the young engineer so far away above her and make it such a solemn affair calling her "Miss Lessing." He had never called her that before. Why, at the Junction he had addressed her as "Kid" and given her a homey, little-girl feeling that put her at her ease. With faltering footsteps she entered the booth and closed the door, saying "Hello" in such a weak little frightened voice that she had to repeat it before it was heard. But then came the hearty voice of her own friendly engineer over the phone:

"Thank goodness! Then it's really you, Hilda Lessing, is it? We certainly have had some hunt. You nervy little kid, you, what have you been doing? Turning detective on your own account and beating the Secret Service to it? Well, I'm proud of you, but I am mighty glad I've found you at last, for we've had all kinds of a scare about you. Your mother came on to see you, you know."

"My mother!" gasped Hilda with delight and relief. "Oh, where is she?"

"She's right here beside me, and she's going to talk to you in a minute, but first I want to tell you something. When I got home just now I found that my mother was gone to Washington on a short trip, so I got her on the phone at once, and she's coming after you right away and going to take you to her hotel with her. You stay right where you are! till she gets there; because she won't know you otherwise, and we don't want to lose you again, you know. We've had all kinds of a time finding you."

"Oh, but I couldn't go to a fine hotel!" gasped Hilda. "I've only my working dress! And I lost my hat and coat running for the train. I'm really not fit —"

"Oh! that doesn't make any difference," came the hearty response. "My mother'll fix you all up. She'll love to do it. You just tell her all about it. She's a peach of a mother, and she loves girls. My sister died when she was a baby, and Mother has always wanted a daughter. She'll just be tickled to death to get hold of you. You'll love her, I know, for she's simply great! I know, for I'm a good judge of mothers. You've got a mighty fine one yourself, and now she wants to talk to you."

Hilda gasped in astonishment and tried to

think of something to say, but the man's voice was gone, and in a minute she heard a shy little "Hello!" in which she hardly recognized her mother's voice.

"Hello!" she said eagerly. "Oh, Mother, is that you? Is it really you?" and suddenly the tears came with a swift rush and drowned her eyes and choked her voice.

"Yes, darling!" came the mother's voice eagerly. "Isn't it wonderful? I was so worried and afraid, with the long journey and that awful woman, and then not finding you! But Mr. Stevens was beautiful. He brought us straight to his lovely home. I don't feel as if we ought to stay here, but he would have it. Are you really all right? Not sick nor hurt nor anything? They have found out through the conductor what a narrow escape from death you had in getting on the train, and I have been so worried about you. Didn't you get hurt at all?"

"Oh, no, Mother, I'm all right," laughed Hilda hysterically, "and I'm so glad to hear your voice. Is Karl with you, too? How great! Oh, I wish I could fly to you! But I've got to stay here for a day or two, they say. They want me for evidence against those people."

"I know, dear child! They have told me. That's all right. Just do as Mrs. Stevens says; I know she must be lovely. I've been talking to her on the phone, and I'm so relieved that there is a woman down there who will be good to you. Mr.

Stevens says we will call up in the morning and make our plans, so don't worry."

"But how did you happen to be here, Mother?"

"Why, I've left that asylum! It was quite impossible to stay. I'll tell you all about it when I see you. I don't know what your Uncle Otto will say when he knows, but I really couldn't keep Karl there! But I'll find something else to do, I'm sure, so don't worry!"

When Hilda came out of the telephone booth there was a tender, shiny look in her eyes that made the officers look away from her quickly as if they had caught a glimpse of some holy vision that was not for stranger eyes; but the sweet-faced woman who was sitting in the chair that Hilda had vacated when she went to the telephone, dwelt with pleased eyes upon the tired young face. So this was the girl who had interested her son. She was glad she was slender and pretty and young, with that look of mingled innocence and strength about her, and not a modern girl with a self-sufficient swagger and a look of having turned the universe inside out and found little in it worth her notice. She had not owned it to herself before, but she had been just a wee bit worried down deep in her heart ever since Dan had spoken of the little girl whose life he had saved, lest she might turn out to be a girl who would try to make much of her hold upon him. But this girl never would, this lovely, modest girl with the high bearing and the look of soul culture in her face. Whoever she was, and wherever she came from, she had a gentle, grave dignity about her that was exceedingly pleasing. Mrs. Stevens liked the shy way in which the girl lifted her serious eyes and studied her face when the Chief introduced her, and she liked the simple deprecatory way in which she dismissed the matter of her impossible garb with a glance down and a smile of apology.

"I am really not fit to go with you, Mrs. Stevens," said the girl. "I would much rather you would send me to a plain boarding house where I shall not mortify you. I haven't even any hat. I pinned this up out of my work apron after I got on the train." She took off the little brown cap and looked at it ruefully, thereby revealing her lovely head of heavy hair, beautiful even in its disarray from the long hard day.

"It is a very clever little cap, my dear," said the lady, examining it curiously, "and a wonderful little girl to be able to evolve it in necessity. Don't worry about your clothes, dear. We'll fix all that up in the morning. You're coming with me now to get a good night's rest. Tomorrow, they tell me, you are to see the President, and you will need to get rested and ready for that. Just play I'm your mother, or your aunt, if you like that better, and come on with me to my hotel."

14

In wonder Hilda found herself seated in a big limousine slipping through the broad streets of Washington, peering out at the looming pillars of the Treasury building, whirling around a corner and up to the door of the great hotel. It was only a glimpse she caught of beautiful halls and corridors as they whisked up in the elevator, and then she was taken into a big cool room opening from a delightful big sitting-room full of easy chairs. A white-tiled bathroom gleamed beyond, a telephone stood under a softly shaded light, a little desk with papers and pens was at hand, and all this elegance was for her alone. Hilda stood in the middle of the room and looked about her with wonder and delight. Then suddenly a vision of her bare little room at the truck farm came to her and she laughed, a sweet, clear gurgle of amusement.

"Excuse me!" she said as she saw Mrs. Stevens's look of surprise. "I was just wondering what Mrs. Schwarz would say if she could see me in this room. Oh, you don't know how — *different* — everything is!"

A tender look softened the woman's eyes, and she came over and kissed the girl almost reverently.

"You dear child!" she murmured. "You must

have been having a very hard time, and one can see you have been brave about it. You must tell me all about it in the morning. But now you must rest. I will get you a few of my things for tonight, and in the morning we will go out and look up some of your own. There is your private bathroom. Perhaps it would rest you to take a bath unless you are too tired. Would you like me to ring for a maid, or would you rather look after yourself?"

"Oh, much rather!" said Hilda, with another of her quaint little gasps. "I should be frightened to death of a maid. And please don't take any trouble for me. I can get along beautifully with what I have."

But Mrs. Stevens went over to her own room, which opened on the other side of the sitting-room, and returned with her arms full. A lovely pale blue silk kimono embroidered in cherry blossoms, a perfect dream of a white nightrobe all dainty with frills of lace and blue ribbons, an ivory brush and comb, and a pair of blue satin slippers with tiny rosettes of pink rosebuds. Hilda went over and looked at each of the articles in amazement after her hostess had kissed her good-night and left her with injunctions to sleep as late in the morning as possible, and not to think of trying to get dressed till she brought her some things. How wonderful and fairy-like it all was! To think that this should have happened to her!

She took her luxurious bath, being a long time about it in spite of her weariness, because it was all such a wonderful experience — the white tub, the hot and cold water in abundance, the scented soap, the big, soft towels. She could not help contrasting it with the tin wash basin on a box at Schwarz's. And then, too, she told herself that she would probably never have such a bath again in a bathroom all her own like this.

She put on the delicate nightrobe, brushed out her lovely hair with the beautiful brush, tried on the blue silk kimono for a brief glimpse of herself in the mirror; then put it back on the chair and crept with a kind of awe into the great white bed that was so soft she felt as if she were floating on a cloud. Then, the very next thing she knew, it was morning! Oh, very late morning, indeed; and Mrs. Stevens was standing by the bed in a charming gown, looking down on her.

"Aren't you ever going to wake up, dear child?" she said smiling. "You've skipped breakfast entirely, and if you don't hurry there won't be any time left for lunch. Come, wake up! I've been out and bought you some things and I'm anxious to see if they fit you."

Dazed and bewildered, Hilda opened her eyes and smiled about her on the wonderful dream that was staying real, and the sweet woman who was talking to her exactly as if she were one of her own family.

The "few things" were lying on the chairs

about the room. There were filmy garments of lingerie, silk stockings and dainty pumps.

"I took one of your shoes along to get the size," explained the lady. "I hope they will fit you. There are three pairs of different styles for you to try on. I hope one of them will fit."

It was wonderful to get dressed up in those beautiful new clothes and see herself looking like a stylish young stranger in the long mirror.

"But I oughtn't to wear them," she said deprecatingly, "for I can never pay for them, you know; and I shall soil them, I'm afraid."

"Don't talk about pay, dear child!" said Mrs. Stevens. "You are my little girl for today, and I buy what I like for you. Besides, didn't you save the life of my dear boy for me? Didn't you risk a great deal to send him word; and didn't you save a lot of other lives and a lot of valuable property, without ever stopping to think of yourself? Isn't it right that you should wear the best that is to be had. Please don't say any more. You'll be perfectly able to pay for clothes such as these after the railroad gets done giving you what they owe you for what you did for them; although I claim the right to buy you what I please today just because I love you for saving my son's life, and because I love you for being what you are — a dear, unspoiled, brave little girl! Now say no more! Get dressed as fast as you can, for we want to make the most of what there is left of the day. You have an appointment to meet the President this afternoon. Word has just come from the Executive Mansion. And tomorrow Dan is going to get off and bring your mother and brother down to see us."

It was all so wonderful and bewildering that Hilda could scarcely keep her head about her. But she managed to get herself dressed in the new garments in an incredibly short space of time, despite strange hooks and girdles and fastenings.

There was nothing about the plain brown rajah silk dress to which Hilda could object as being showy or too grand for one in her position, for it was simple and dark, and rather plain in its make, but it had an air of distinction, as though made by an artist in clothes, and designed purposely for her. The cut of the long, lovely lines on her slender figure, the exquisite pressing of the perfect pleats, the curve of the transparent sleeves, the finish of the girdle and neck, all proclaimed its high origin.

The little hat to go with it was a fine milan braid in tricorne shape, with just a rim of brown wing above the edge of the rolling brim, and was most becoming when put upon the brown head.

"I tried to get the shape as near the one you made as possible, because that was so becoming to you," said the elder woman with a smile as she watched the girl put the finishing touches to her toilet.

Mrs. Stevens had forgotten nothing: gloves,

umbrella and shiny leather handbag with a pretty gold clasp. There was even a suitcase in which to put away her old garments from the eyes of the chambermaid.

"You have been so very good to me!" said Hilda, turning from the survey of her new self in the glass. "How can I ever thank you?"

"It is sweet enough thanks to see the look in your pretty eyes, dear. Now, shall we go down to the dining-room?"

That was a wonderful day to Hilda, a day to be remembered all her life. After lunch they went in the big car shopping, and Mrs. Stevens insisted upon purchasing a lot more pretty clothes, and a trunk in which to put them. She said she wanted the pleasure of doing some of the things she would have done for her own daughter if she had lived. She said it so sincerely that Hilda had not the heart to gainsay her, although she wondered in her heart what she should do with all the lovely things when she went back into her workaday world once more and had no place to wear them? However, the beautiful lady would have her way.

The last stop of the shopping trip was at a jewelry shop, where Mrs. Stevens fairly took Hilda's breath away by purchasing a tiny gold wrist watch and a small pin in the form of a crescent of pearls with one tiny dewdrop of a diamond at the tip.

"They are just to remind you of my deep gratitude for saving my dear son," she said as she fastened the pin on Hilda's dress.

Then they drove down the broad avenue to the White House, and the great iron gates opened to them without a hindrance. So it was that Hilda Lessing entered into the charmed spot where the eyes of all the women of the land turn wistfully now and then, and long to enter in. She not only was allowed to enter now, but had been bidden by the great man of the land himself.

Hilda had a glimpse of the big room where the great and small gather to meet the great; and a fleeting view of several other rooms where more intimate audiences are held; and then all at once she was in the genial presence of the President himself, and he was looking at her with those friendly, keen eyes and saying gracious words to her.

Afterward she could not remember what she answered to his kindly questions, nor whether she had the sense to thank him for the medal on her breast. She looked with wonder at it back in her room when she laid it carefully in the little velvet-lined leather case where it belonged, and realized that she had won this honor just by being faithful to the right and loyal to her country and her flag.

They finished the perfect day by dinner in the great hotel dining-room and a drive in the car to a fine old place in the suburbs, where there were nice people and beautiful music. Mrs. Stevens made her wear a lovely fluffy pink and blue affair of chiffon delicately picked out with crystal beads here and there. She felt like a girl in a dream. But the crowning wonder of the whole day was that few minutes she had spent in the White House. She kept going back again and again with a thrill of her heart to the memory.

She thought she never would get to sleep that night with all the wonderful things she had to think about, but sleep dropped down upon her unawares; and morning rose upon her bright with anticipation, for she remembered with her waking thought that her mother and brother were coming that day. She tried to hide from herself how glad she was that the young engineer was coming, too, until the joy of her heart just clamored to get out and express itself to her, and she could keep it back no longer with any reproofs.

"Well, why shouldn't I be glad, just once?" she smiled to herself in the glass as she arranged her bronze braids with special care. "He saved my life, and it will be nice to see him once more and say another thank you again. Of course, I know he is rich, and I probably will never see him again after I go back to Chicago, but it isn't wrong to have a good time just for once. I'm not silly. I shan't get a notion he is in love with me or anything," and she smiled wistfully at herself in the glass.

Somehow life seemed a great deal more bearable now that she was away from the Schwarzes and there was a prospect of seeing her mother. Maybe they could find work together somewhere and be able to live at home once more. Wouldn't that be great!

She went out to meet her hostess with a smiling face.

Hilda had thought that no day could quite equal in wonder the one that had just passed, but she found this new one thrilled her anew, and after all surpassed anything she had yet experienced.

The travelers arrived soon after they had finished breakfast, and Hilda was so glad to see her mother and brother that she forgot all the transformation that had happened to herself, and didn't even see the delight and surprise in the eyes of the young man as he looked at her for the first time in the hotel sitting-room.

His mother saw it, however, and watching, turned with a shade of anxiety toward the quiet little woman in black who was mother to this sweet stray girl, to see what she was like. Perhaps the relief she felt when she saw the lines of fineness and strength in the tired sad face gave cordiality to her own greeting as she stepped forward to be introduced.

But perhaps the greatest surprise of all was when Hilda turned to see her engineer, whom, it will be remembered, she had seen but once at close range (except a distant fleeting view of his head and shoulders in the cab of his engine) and whom she remembered always in blue jean overalls.

He was dressed now in the full uniform of an officer of the United States Army; and fine and handsome did he look as he stood ready to salute her, pausing to admire his little friend, whom he had not known was so beautiful until his mother had put on the finishing touches of suitable garments.

There was unmistakable admiration in both pairs of eyes as the two young people stood facing each other for a moment, a flash of something recognized from each to the other, and then they came back to themselves. Hilda, with a flame of scarlet in her cheeks and a swift drooping of her shy eyelids as she realized that she had been letting her thoughts sit unrebuked upon her face.

It was young Karl who brought them all to their senses again. He had been quietly in the background, had gone through the introductions with fairly creditable efficiency, and was now standing at the window looking out.

"Oh, gee!" he remarked to himself, eagerly. "Is that the Capitol up there on the hill? Say, Hilda, let's go out and look at it!"

"Why of course!" said Mrs. Stevens in her easy pleasant voice. "That's what we are all going to do right away. Unless your mother feels too tired, in which case she and I will stay here and rest and talk. Are you too tired, Mrs. Lessing?"

"Oh, I'm not too tired," said the other woman with a bright smile that reminded one of Hilda. "I'm not tired at all now I've found my dear girl. I feel as if I never would be tired again. But I'm too shabby. I had to come away without any preparation whatever, and, of course, I had no idea of coming to a place like this. Now we are here the children must see the nation's Capitol. They might not have another opportunity. But no one need stay with me. I'll just sit by the window in this lovely comfortable chair and look out while you go. It's very good of you to take them. But I couldn't think of going out looking like this."

"Oh, is that all?" smiled Mrs. Stevens happily. "Why, I've plenty of things, a whole trunk full, and I think we are about of a size. Of course, you will want to change after traveling so far this warm weather. Just come with me and we'll see if we can find anything that fits you."

She led the frightened little mother away to her own room. But Mrs. Lessing did not stay frightened long. The other woman was too cordial and spoke too charmingly of Hilda for her to hold her diffidence; and before they knew it they had forgotten what they came for and were sitting hand-in-hand talking about their two children and how they had saved each other's lives, until Karl, staring impatiently out of the window, grew quite in despair. For there behind him was his own sister, transformed into a society lady unexpectedly by just clothes, so that he couldn't feel quite at home with her, even though she did hug him and choke him almost to death; and there was that perfectly good young engineer transformed into a perfectly stunning soldier — officer, too — and though just as friendly as could be but a minute before, now altogether oblivious of his existence. And there was the Capitol gleaming in the sunshine up there on the hill calling his impatient feet to climb. Karl couldn't understand it. Things seemed to have started out pretty well, and now to have come to this sudden standstill!

He turned around to appeal to Hilda, and found her and the young soldier deep in conversation. They were telling each other what had happened at Schwarz's after Hilda had telephoned about the plan to blow up the bridge. They were sitting on the couch quite close together and they were telling it into each other's eyes. They didn't seem to notice Karl at all, though he came and sat quite near to hear all about the powder and the spies. The young officer got out something from his pocket and showed it to Hilda. That little old red scarf! His old scarf that he used to wear to school! Now what was there in that? What in the world did he want to carry that around for? He was asking Hilda if he might keep it, and he was putting it back in his pocket again carefully as if it were something precious. What could he want of a faded old scarf like that? Such a hot day, too!

Then the soldier put his hand over Hilda's and looked in her eyes and talked in low tones. He told her what a wonderful little girl she had been, and Karl felt left out and went back to the window. He sat there in a kind of impatient disgust watching the people passing on the street below. Did all nice things have to be stopped and end in such silly ways? Would they never start for the Capitol? What difference did it make what people wore?

At last the two mothers came back, but what had been done to his mother? She was transformed!

15

She was dressed in a soft clinging black gown and a big transparent black hat; and she looked young, younger than he ever remembered seeing her look before. He had a feeling that the earth was reeling under him and he might never dare to be intimate with his mother again. He went up to her shyly, looked in her face, touched her hand, and she stooped and kissed him. There were tears in her eyes! Had that other woman been making her cry? But no, they were happy tears, for she was smiling. They were all smiling! What did they see to smile about? Was it funny to be so long getting ready to go to a place?

Then Hilda brought her medal and told them about her visit to the President and he forgot all about his impatience. Here, indeed, was something to smile about! He was proud of his sister! *His sister!* He looked at her wonderingly and drew himself up. To think she had done all that! And she was beautiful, yes, she was! He had never noticed it before, but she was really beautiful, and she looked fine beside that nice big soldier.

"Do you know, Dan," said Mrs. Stevens, "Mrs. Lessing used to be the principal of a high school before she was married? I've been telling her that I believe your father knows of just the right position for her. You know he has been looking for a woman fitted to fill that vacancy left by the death of Mrs. Clemons. It pays well and has the added inducement of being work that the Government needs badly just now. Do you think that might work?"

"Indeed, I do!" said the young man with an appreciative flash in his eyes for the mother who had stepped in and done the very thing for this stranger that he had hoped she would do when he brought her here. "Telephone Father about it tonight, won't you, Mother, before he hunts up someone else? Then they could live in Philadelphia and you could put them onto things and help them to know nice people. And Miss Lessing could finish her education."

He smiled at Hilda.

"That is a beautiful dream," said Hilda smiling back, "but you mustn't turn my head with such ideas. I know a thing like that could never come true for me."

"I don't see why not!" said the young soldier with a gentle intonation. "You deserve anything good the world has to offer."

The sweet color swept in a pink wave over Hilda's fair face, but Karl suddenly supplied an antidote to the tension of the moment:

"Oh, gee! I'd like to live in Philadelphia! That is — after I've seen the Capitol and a few other places!" The sentence ended in a patient sigh, and they all laughed at the obvious hint.

"Well, now we're going to see the Capitol at once!" said Mrs. Stevens pleasantly. "And it really isn't late at all yet. We'll have time to see a number of places; and then after lunch we can drive to Arlington and Mount Vernon if you like."

It was while they wandered through the grounds of Washington's beautiful home at Mount Vernon that Hilda and Stevens had their talk. The others were in the house studying the wonderful old rooms filled with their fine mahogany furniture, quaint candlesticks and many queer, old-fashioned relics.

The two young people wandered down to the tomb and gazed for a moment in silence through the iron grating, and read the inscription which commemorates the life and death of the Father of his Country.

"Do you know, I think it is quite fitting that you should come here just now," said the young man. "You are a true daughter of a democracy of which George Washington was the father. If he were alive he, too, would give you his blessing for the loyal way in which you have served your country in the face of great peril to yourself. You are as much a soldier in this war as I am. You should wear a uniform, too, by rights, and have a commission. In a few days I am going to France to do my part in this great war, I hope; but it is very unlikely that I shall have opportunity to do anything great in comparison to what you have done for the cause. You are only a young girl, but you have been as brave and true and quick as any man could have been. And the great man who lies in that tomb would have been the first one to have told you so if he were living."

They had turned from the tomb and were walking down the close-cut lawn to the terrace overlooking the river. Hilda lifted her shining eyes to the young soldier's face and spoke eagerly:

"But I could not have done anything at all if it had not been for you. In the first place, I shouldn't have been alive to do it if you had not saved me from that express train! And I should not have known enough to do anything if you had not talked about spies and told me to send word to Washington if I found any. Of course, when I got hold of that suitcase I had to bring it myself. There was no other way to get it here safely. Anybody would have done it. Don't you see, after all, it was really you who did every bit of it?"

"No, you sweet child, I don't see anything but you and your true loyal soul in your eyes," he answered, smiling down at her. "Let us sit down under this tree. I want to ask you a few questions."

There was something in his voice and manner that made Hilda suddenly conscious of herself and her extraordinary situation, and brought the pink to her cheeks and the shining wonder to her eyes. She sat down on the grassy bank in a tumult of amazement at herself. Here was she, the erstwhile kitchen maid of the Schwarz truck farm, attired in beautiful and modish garments and sitting at her ease with a son of wealth and culture, nay, a soldier of rank and accomplishments! How had it come about? How was it that she was not covered with confusion before him, she a shy little school girl who had never been into society? Were all rich and cultured people like this if you only got to know them well? Perhaps, if he had not been an engineer she never would have known him at all. For, although he might have saved her life, yet she felt sure she would never have felt so free with him, nor confided in him as she did, if he had been dressed like a gentleman instead of having on that old blue blouse and greasy cap. It somehow made him just a man, and swept away all class distinctions that would have made her shy. And yet, how perverse was the human heart! Now that she knew him she liked him better dressed like a gentleman! It had not been the clothes after all. It was just that he was a true gentleman all the time, whatever he wore, only at first there had been no marks of the barriers of wealth to keep her from knowing the man.

All this swept vaguely through her mind as she settled herself on the velvety turf and leaned back against the old tree trunk, looking down at the calm, steady river flowing by. Down there, close to the water, another girl in a white dress with a flutter of pink ribbons, was walking with a soldier. Hilda's heart swelled with sudden pride. She had a soldier, too, just for the day. She need not look at that other girl with envy. She was looking well, and having a beautiful companionship with one who could stand with the best of the land. It was a wonderful thing to have come to her. Of course, it was not to last. He would go on, away, to France, and probably she would never see him again for years, perhaps never! But she would have it in her memory to take out and think about and perhaps tell — no, she would never tell! It should be hid in her heart. She would tell how the President had once talked with her; but this young man — this was her own beautiful memory to keep in her heart all the days of her life. There might be other Presidents, but there would never be another like this one! Her cheeks glowed a little deeper with the thought of what this admission must mean. She turned to look at him with sudden realization that he had been silent a long time, and discovered that he was watching her. Then their eyes met and his face burst into the wonderful smile that seemed to flood her very soul. No, there would never be another like him, and she must keep the memory of every word and look in her heart for the time when she would walk her quiet way alone again.

"I have been wondering," he said, with what

seemed to her great irrelevance, and still looking earnestly at her, "whether you have a lot of friends in France to whom you are writing?"

"Oh, no!" she said blankly. The conversation seemed to have been suddenly diverted from the personal to the general, and she sat up a little straighter and tried to realize that she was only a casual acquaintance with whom he was trying to be pleasant for the day, and, of course, it was very good of him. "Oh, no! Karl is my only brother. We hadn't anybody to go."

"But you had other friends, school friends and neighbors, didn't you?"

"Oh, yes!" said Hilda, with a little sigh of indifference. "The boys in school enlisted, or were drafted, but I never knew any of them very well. We lived two miles from the high school. I had to go on the trolley. Mother didn't like me to be out late, and I always went right home to help her. I didn't go to any of the high school dances, and, of course, I didn't get acquainted. I knew them all, but just to speak to, not anything more. There wasn't time. I always wanted all my extra time for study because I wanted to get ahead, so I could teach and do a lot of things for Mother. Mother didn't care for the neighbors around us. She hoped we'd be able to move away to another part of the city soon, so I would have the kind of friends she liked for me. But Father died and everything was changed."

There was a lingering look of tenderness in his

glance before he took up his questions again:

"Then I wonder if you could find time to write to me while I'm away?"

She turned to him with surprise and joy in her face, and her voice almost trembled as she spoke:

"*I* write to *you?*" Then the sunny light slowly faded out of her eyes and renunciation began to settle down about her firm little mouth.

"I should love to," she said wistfully. "But I guess that wouldn't be right."

"Why not?" he demanded. "Is there someone else?"

"Oh, no!" she opened her eyes wide in amusement and her laugh rippled out. Then sobering: "No, but you surely know there is a great difference between us. You belong to the rich and great; to the people who know things and do things and — *are* things! But I am just a little school girl who has got to earn her living. We are very very poor since my father died! You and your mother have been very kind to me, but I'm quite sure she wouldn't want you writing to a girl like me."

"I'm quite sure she would!" he burst forth eagerly. "She thinks you are a girl among a thousand. She told me so herself. And what is money! I've got plenty of money, but I would rather throw it all away than let it separate me from congenial friends. Come now, you'll have to give me a better reason than that if you want to cut me out of your circle of friendship."

"Oh, I don't want to do that at all!" she cried in distress. "But — why — don't you realize that I've been a hired girl on a truck farm! And you are an officer in the United States Army; and the son of the president of a great railroad; and the friend of the President of the United States, and a whole lot of other great friends. You've been through college, and are going to be a great man. I'm only an ignorant little school girl who will never have much of a chance to learn to be anything."

"Nonsense!" cried the young soldier proudly. "You've been a loyal American citizen! What does it matter what else you've been? Isn't this a democracy? Don't we believe in real things? What difference how you have served so long as you've had the fineness and the heart to serve? And as for being and doing anything, Hilda, do you know that there is a cordon of Secret Service men stretched all around that truck farm today just on account of you? Do you know that Schwarz and his men can't stir without the United States Government knowing exactly what each is doing? Don't you know that the officer who comes in an aeroplane will be watched for and tracked next week, if he tries to come again, and it will likely be discovered just where else he goes and who he is, and who he is working for, and whether there are other truck farms that he visits. And it is all through your quick, brave action that this is possible. By the way, I didn't tell you that down under the iron lid below your cabbages I saw hundreds of guns stored and ready for quick handing out. And do you know that very likely before many days the Government will know just where other stores are kept, the powder and the dynamite you heard them talk about, and who are the ones employed to blow up munition plants and ship-yards, and place bombs under bridges and in the holds of loaded ships? As soon as they have them just where they want them and find out every-body that is in the frame-up they will all be in jail, Schwarz and all his gang, too. This information has come through you, and yet, in spite of all the honor that has been put upon you, and is going to be done you, you are not the least bit conceited. You are making yourself as small and humble as can be. Don't you think I know fine-ness when I see it? You may have worked in a kitchen, but you have the soul of a queen, and — of a soldier! Yes, you have! No man could have done a finer, braver thing than you have done! I mean it! And I want you for my friend. Come, will you write to me? Unless, perhaps you think that I'm the one that's unworthy? Is that it?"

"Oh, no!" she put out her hand with a quick little protest. "Oh, no!"

He took her hand gravely, gently, in his own, looking down and marveling at its shapeliness and supple strength.

"Well, then, will you write to me and try me out for a friend?"

Hilda's eyes answered for her before her lips could frame the words, and a sweet look of joy, like one who had received a high calling, shone in her face. They had entirely forgotten that they were sitting with clasped hands, until Karl's voice pierced through the shrubbery, sweetly imperious, like one who was being hindered on the greatest occasion of his life:

"Hilda! Hilda! Where are you? Hurry up, you two! We're going back to the hotel and we're going to have ice-cream again for dinner! And then we're going to a movie!"

16

Through the next few days Hilda moved like one in a beautiful dream, from which she expected soon to wake into the regular drab-colored world where she belonged. But she dreamed with a smile on her lips and joy in her eyes. She was as lovely and unconscious of self as a girl could be, and more and more young Daniel Stevens's mother was drawn to her.

The young man had gone to his camp, and Hilda's mother had received a summons to come to Philadelphia to try out for the position which Mr. Stevens senior had recommended her for, and had taken Karl with her, wishing to arrange for his school in case she was accepted.

Hilda was detained by the Secret Service for a few days until a further investigation could be made. The officer of the aeroplane could not be located as yet, and a great deal depended upon his identification. It was decided that she should stay with Mrs. Stevens a little longer.

So the dream wandered on for more beautiful days, filled with rides and walks and sight-seeing, glimpses into lovely homes and churches, meetings with delightful people; a week-end with the young soldier up again from camp, and the delightful senior Stevens down from Philadelphia.

The two young people, set free for the time being from all thought of difference or class distinction, conscious of the approval of their elders, grew whole months in the matter of friendship as they strolled about Washington. They wandered into many of the historic and beautiful spots where a visitor may go. Yet afterwards perhaps their strongest impression was rather of words and glances than of stately halls or paintings of historic value.

Hilda was summoned one morning to look at some photographs. Did they resemble the man who came in an aeroplane, she was asked? She was quite sure they did. She studied each of them carefully. They were small snapshots, two of them taken in a crowd, one on the deck of a departing steamship. One without his hateful moustache. Always to look at them gave her that chill that she had felt when that stranger had told Mrs. Schwarz to make it known that she was his property, "She belongs to me! Understand?" How those words rang in her ears! The night after she had looked at the pictures she lay awake and thought it all over. Were those really pictures of the man, or did she only imagine it because she was all wrought up over what she had gone through? How much responsibility was upon her!

It seemed that the man whose picture she had been shown was a noted German who had been close to diplomatic circles, and had moved unsuspected for years among the most loyal of Americans. Of late there had been whispers about him, vague and indefinite. He had been reported as having gone back to Germany at the time when Von Bernstorff was recalled. Rumor also had reported him in Mexico. There were no proofs, but many indications that he was the moving spirit in German intrigue and propaganda, and yet he was like the proverbial flea, no one could put a finger on him. If he could be found and his identity proved with that of the air-man of the truck farm it meant much in the affairs of the nation and the world. To think that she, insignificant as she was, should all unwittingly have come to be mixed up in such great things! It frightened her when she took time in the watches of the night to think about it.

There was another thing that was troublous to think about, and that was the fact that in spite of the careful watch set about the truck farm, Schwarz and his wife had disappeared; dropped out of existence as it were in the night! Of course, there had been time for them to leave before Hilda reached Washington with her report and set the machinery of the Government in action; and then, too, the nature of the espionage kept about the place was necessarily at a distance until such time as they should be ready to round up the whole gang. But it was annoying to feel that the chief actors in the scene had disappeared so unaccountably. Hilda spent hours thinking about it whenever she was left to herself. Had there been an underground tunnel through which the two had departed in disguise? Had they opened her suitcase after she left and discovered that she had taken the other one with her? Would they perhaps lie in wait for her some day if she chanced to come in their way, and get their revenge? She shuddered and turned away from the thought as quite impossible in a plain, commonsense world, with sunshine and beautiful things all about; and yet it left a shadow in her heart that sometimes gave her an unpleasant sensation. She wished the Schwarzes were safely interned or imprisoned somewhere. In the days that followed, however, she had no room for gloom. Daniel Stevens came often to Washington for a few hours to be with them, and occasionally she and his mother motored to the camp and spent a pleasant half day going about with him. And then, just the very day that the Secret Service people had told her that she might go to Philadelphia now if she chose, as they would not need her further until they had some track of either the Schwarzes or the air-man, word came from the young soldier that he was to leave for France in a few hours.

Somehow Hilda had not realized until that afternoon of farewell what a terrible thing war was. It had not come to her until then that this young man who was becoming so much to her was going out to face death perhaps, just as all those others had gone. He was to be in the forefront of things, helping to reconstruct railroads, and run the first trains over ground that was but just recovered from the enemy. He would be subject to work under fire. There would be terrible danger everywhere and the enemy would be — millions of Schwarzes! led by men like the air-man! Cruel, selfish, beastly, fiendish! Her first thoughts at Platt's Crossing about the American boys marching out to meet long lines of Germans returned to her with vivid horror, for now it was her true friend, Daniel Stevens, with his fine bearing, his merry brown eyes, and his firm strong chin that looked as though it would never give up, who was going out to the struggle. Her heart quailed and her lips faltered as she gave her hand for farewell. Her face was white with the pain of it, and the possibilities that had flashed before her mind in that second.

"There's one thing I want you to promise me, Hilda Lessing," he said, looking earnestly into her eyes. "I don't like the thought that those Schwarzes and that captain are floating around loose, and knowing that you have been on their track. They are liable to turn up somewhere and get it back on you. I want you to promise me that you will never get into any cab or automobile that anybody sends after you unless you know the driver and are perfectly sure of him! I want you to promise you won't go out alone at night, nor answer any strange letters or appeals or anything that might lure you into their power! Remember, they have your suitcase and by this time in all probability they know that you were the one that put the Government wise to them. The fact that all three have apparently dropped out of existence leaving no tracks behind, shows that they know we are onto them. Now, will you promise? I shan't feel safe about you one minute unless you do."

"Of course," said Hilda, a flood of emotion choking her voice. To think that he should care! That he should be so thoughtful of her!

"You'll keep pretty close to your mother — or mine, won't you?"

"Oh, yes!" said Hilda, the pretty color coming and going in her round cheeks. "As close as I can and attend to my work."

"You won't take any risks, will you? Because — well — because —"

He was looking at her with such a world of meaning in his eyes that her own drooped before his gaze and her heart leaped with joy that he should care so much about her. The Schwarzes at that moment seemed a thing far away and not at all to be feared, since he cared so much. His caring shut her away from all fear like a beautiful robe of protection.

There was so much joy, after all, mingled with the pain of the parting that on the way to Philadelphia Mrs. Stevens studied the girl's face in some doubt. Did she care after all for the boy who had gone away to the war? She knew the look on her boy's face and she knew he was deeply interested in this girl. Was the girl as much interested, or was she just a good friend who had not yet awakened to the great things of life? Well, it was just as well, for the child would not have to suffer so much. Yet as she studied the sweet face with the dreamy eyes that looked without seeing the flying landscape the mother wondered after all if there were not something deeper behind that sweet smile than just a passing happiness for the pleasant times that were suddenly surrounding her after the hard summer. She wondered if Hilda were not even then remembering the look in the soldier's eyes as he said good-bye. The future would have to tell! She was very well satisfied to have her boy interested in a girl like this. Sweet and strong and unselfish, with fine ambitions, and a will to accomplish them. She was going to have a good deal of pleasure herself with the girl and her mother. She had always wanted a daughter, and this girl was charming. How she would like to do beautiful things for her! Yet she knew in her heart that both mother and girl were too self-respecting to allow much to be done for them. It would just have to be a case of being a dear friend and slipping in help where it would seem perfectly natural; and she had to confess, too, that she liked them all the better for that.

Thus Hilda, with pleasant thoughts, and

much wonder in her heart over the way things were turning out, went on her way back to Philadelphia. She could not help contrasting herself with the little girl in the brown denim cap who traveled that way alone so short a time before, when she caught a glimpse of herself in a mirror of the parlor car. The slim elegant little figure that sat back luxuriously in the big chair, perfect in every dainty appointment of her toilet and her traveling accessories, seemed such a contrast to the Schwarzes' hired girl running away to tell the President, that she laughed aloud.

Her companion turned wondering eyes upon her.

"I was just thinking, Mrs. Stevens, how astonished Mrs. Schwarz would be if she could see me now!" she said with a little ripple of laughter.

"Dear child!" said the older woman, "I hope she will never see you again!" and she put out a protecting hand to touch the girl.

Hilda turned to her with a quick, loving glance.

"And how good you were to me that night in Washington, taking me to that lovely hotel when I looked such a fright! Oh! You must have been so ashamed of me!"

"My dear!" said the woman gently. "You wore a lovely soul in your eyes. What did anything else matter? Besides, you're mistaken about your looks that night. You had had a hard trip, of course, and were a bit mussed, but the first thing

I noticed about you was the pretty contour of the little cap you improvised so cleverly. Your dress was neat and simple and fitted well. There was nothing noticeably out of place about you anywhere, so put that out of your mind forever. Now, tell me what are your plans for the winter? If I am not mistaken it is almost time for you to register at the university if you expect to be a student there this year."

The journey was all too brief for the delightful plans they had to talk about, and when they reached Philadelphia, there was the big car waiting with her mother inside, and Karl sitting with the chauffeur in front. The winter looked very bright to Hilda as she watched the lights of the city whirl by, and realized that this was to be her new home.

17

Hilda entered into her studies at the university with a zest that not many students could equal.

"Just to think, Mother, how dreadful everything was last spring when I graduated from high school, and didn't see any way to go to Normal. And now I'm in college! I never dreamed of college! Everything has been so wonderful. It was worth going through that experience at Schwarz's just to have all this, wasn't it? I suppose that's the way all troubles will look when we get to heaven, don't you?"

"I don't know," said the mother with a wistful smile. "I haven't been able yet to think of that truck farm for you without a shudder. I'm glad you can look at it that way; but I keep thinking of a lot of awful things that might have happened. I certainly am thankful and glad that I have you here safe and sound. I'm glad you are back from Washington, too, although I wanted you to have that beautiful time there with Mrs. Stevens, and it was wonderful of her to do what she did; but I kept thinking that perhaps those dreadful men were lurking around somewhere watching for you. It seems to me now as if I was crazy to have allowed you to go off by yourself just because your Uncle Otto said there was no other way. I'm sure there were a thousand other ways if I had bestirred myself; but I was just paralyzed for the time with the thought that the house and the money and everything was gone."

"I know, Mother, you weren't to blame. There wasn't any other way then, either. There just wasn't. But I've wondered sometimes why Uncle Otto thought it would do. He knew Father never would have allowed us to go to such places — or at least I don't think he would. Would he have, Mother?"

She searched her mother's averted face anxiously. Somehow her experiences of the last few weeks had opened her eyes and awakened many questions that had never troubled her before.

"Your father was a very busy man, Hilda," evaded her mother. "He let me do a great deal as I pleased — that is, with my own," she added thoughtfully. "You know I had quite a little money of my own when I was married."

Hilda eyed her with new interest.

"You had? Then what became of it?"

"I don't quite know," answered her mother with a troubled look. "I allowed your father to put it in his business at one time, but he said he had paid it all back and it was in a separate account. Just a few days before he died he said he was going to bring me all the papers. I had put it in the business on that condition, for I had heard of so many people doing that and then being left penniless when something happened. I didn't want you and Karl to be left this way. I wanted to keep my money for you. He told me that the papers were all down m the safe and he would bring them up the next day. But the next day he forgot, and then the next he was gone! Your Uncle Otto says he doesn't know anything about it. He says the money was never put in the business and that there was some mistake. He thinks your father used it for a private speculation and didn't want me to know."

"Would Father have done that, Mother?" asked Hilda in a low, troubled voice.

Her mother turned hastily away and wiped two tears from her eyes.

"I don't know, Hilda!" she said quietly a minute afterward. "Your father was reserved about most things, and sometimes a little overbearing. You know that yourself. But I thought — he was perfectly honest —"

"Well, I think it's Uncle Otto!" declared the girl decidedly, "and I think I'm done with him. Mother, he must have known what those Schwarzes were when he sent me there; or else he didn't know, and he told a lie when he said they were his friends. Mother, have you ever thought that perhaps Uncle Otto is interested in the German Government? He couldn't be a —"

"A spy, you mean? Child! I hope not! Oh, if I thought we were disgraced in that way in our own country, the country my father loved, and my grandfather died for!"

"Well, there, Mother! Uncle Otto is nothing to

us. If he's a spy, we'll change our names and take your maiden name. We'll show the Government that we are not spies, anyway. And come, smooth out your face and smile, Mother, dear! What's money, anyway! We've got enough now to start on and when I get through college and can go to work I'll show Uncle Otto somehow what a big mistake he made. Until then — goodby, Uncle Otto!" and she kissed her pink finger tips and blew a fluted greeting to an imaginary uncle in the distance.

The Lessings were located most delightfully in a charming little apartment but three blocks away from the Stevens mansion. Mrs. Stevens had been vigilant in securing it and in helping to make it delightful, insisting upon lending a lot of old mahogany furniture and pretty rugs and other things which she said were only in the way and would have to be stored unless they took care of them for the winter; and then as a last touch that they could not well resist, she asked the privilege of furnishing Hilda's room herself with some of the things she would have given a daughter of her own if she had one. She was always harking back to how Hilda saved her son's life, until Hilda told her she had paid her many times over for the little she did toward it, and he had done far more for her. But still she would not be denied. So the crowning beauty of the little seven-rooms-and-a-bath was the room that Hilda had chosen. The furniture was ivory white with simple lines and wide low curves in bed and chair and dressing table. The floor was covered with a huge Chinese rug in blue and tawny yellow, how costly Hilda could only guess. Its blue was repeated in the velvet of a big soft couch, and a cozy round fat chair, in the soft silk of the inner curtains, the fringed shaded candles on her dressing table, and in the blue and white satin eiderdown that puffed at the foot of the bed. The brushes and toilet articles were all silver backed and monogrammed, and there was a wonderful white bookcase filled with beautifully bound books, and a darling white desk with all sorts of mysterious drawers and cubby holes and a lot of desk paraphernalia in blue leather. On the walls were two or three fine pictures, and when Hilda saw it for the first time after it was finished she felt like a queen with a palace all new made for her.

It was a beautiful winter from beginning to end, except for the anxiety that filled the air everywhere on account of the war. Mrs. Lessing was interested in her work, and gradually the worn, tired lines were smoothing away from her sweet face and giving way to calm. Hilda was immersed in her studies, satisfied with nothing but perfection in her preparation for classes, delighted with her explorations into the world of literature and science, happy in her home, and shyly thrilled with the letters that came to her from over the seas. It was her recreation to sit by the lovely white desk under the light of the blue shaded candles and write long, wise, bright answers to them; and the thickness and frequency of his letters showed that hers were appreciated by the young soldier at the front.

For he was at the front, that was the worst of it — and the glory of it, too. That was why each letter brought a breathless moment of fear before it was opened and read, lest some terrible thing had happened to him. That was why the days when the letters came were so full of song and uplift because he was still all right. Just friends, grand good friends, Hilda told herself they were, nor letting herself question her heart any further.

Mrs. Stevens had been lovely to them. In addition to helping them get settled in their new apartment she interested herself in putting Karl in school, and seeing that Hilda entered the university under the very best possible conditions. She often sent the car around for their use, and came herself for a few minutes as if they were old family friends, quite informally, although Hilda knew from the few days spent in the Stevens home before they found the right apartment that Mrs. Stevens was a woman of great consequence in the city. Her time was more than full and her friends were many. The demands upon her were unceasing. There were clubs and Red Cross and Emergency Aid and numerous other organizations, religious, civic and social, that claimed her constantly. The rich and great came to her and begged for a share in her interest. Yet she had always time for her home and the friends who were near her heart. That she had chosen to make Hilda and her mother of that charmed circle of inner friends was a constant joy and wonderment to Hilda. Often and often she reflected how much the mother and son were alike in this respect; and it never once occurred to her that the charm was in her own lovely natural self and in her sweet mother. She laid it to their goodness of heart that they were so kind to quiet, shy people far beneath their station socially.

As the winter progressed, more and more Mrs. Stevens seemed drawn to Hilda and her mother. She planned to take them to lectures and to great concerts. They had a standing invitation to attend the Saturday evening orchestra concerts, and here a new world of enjoyment opened up to Hilda which lifted her to the seventh heaven of delight. She felt when one of those concerts was over as if she must fling herself down at the feet of God and thank Him for having made melody in the world.

It was not a gay season, of course, on account of the war, but there were many little gatherings, quiet and for a purpose, where a cup of tea and a knitting bag were the only excitement — sometimes, as sugar grew scarce, even without the cup of tea. To these Hilda and her mother were often bidden; and as often as their other engagements permitted they went. Mrs. Lessing, to her surprise, forgot her almost painful embarrassment at the thought of going into this kind of society and found congenial acquaintances. She held her own, too, in the conversations, and often her quiet, wise remarks caused the other women to defer to her on questions that perplexed them. Mrs. Stevens reflected that there was nothing of which to be ashamed in the mother of the girl her son admired.

They were keeping house in their tiny apartment, and enjoying it immensely. They had found a woman nearby who would come in to cook the dinners at night and clean up once a week. Karl bought his lunch at school, where a hot meal was served every day for a small sum, and there really was little else to be done. Hilda was almost ideally happy. She could scarcely believe she was the same girl who had gone to Platt's Crossing to do housework only a few short months before. As she went cheerily about the little white-tiled kitchen of the apartment washing out her dish towels on the nights when the hired woman could not stay to finish, her heart would be just bursting into song to remember those awful days at the truck farm while she worked under the cruel lash of Mrs. Schwarz. How strange and far away and tragic it all seemed, as if it had happened to somebody else. Strange how those Schwarzes had disappeared! Maybe they got on a submarine somehow and went over to Germany. That certainly was where they belonged, not in free, beautiful America!

Then came a sad and anxious time when a big drive was on in France and no letters came from the wanderer. Mrs. Stevens called up or ran in daily to see if Hilda had had any word, and tried to keep a brave, smiling face; but Hilda could see that she was anxious. It was then that Hilda went to her room and, dropping upon her knees beside the white bed, prayed with all her heart, sobbing as she prayed, that her dear friend, her brave soldier boy, might be kept safe from harm. Quite often she brought out her little Bible and read, searching for comfort through the promises of God.

"The angel of the Lord encampeth round about them that fear Him and delivereth them," she read over and over again, catching at it gladly with her spirit in her eyes. Surely that was for him. He feared God and loved Him. Only in his last letter he had said how when he was going out to battle there was always the great thought that very soon he might be facing God. He had written much of how different life looked from the point of view of the battlefield; how small things fell away and there remained only the great things, like right and wrong, sin and forgiveness, and the love of God. He had said that the dear people at home seemed like a strong rock on which he was leaning, and that he knew they were praying for him, and that helped. Again and again she read that letter over and then knelt and poured out her young soul in agony and strength for him, as if she would take hold of God with all her might and force Him to attend to her plea brought in the words of His own promise. Day after day she prayed and read His promises, and day after day went by without word.

All the power of the father, who was a great man in the world of men with much influence at headquarters, was brought to bear upon the matter. Anxious cablegrams slipped through the great waters to the other side, and still no satisfactory answer. All was confusion and congestion in the Department of Intelligence. The battle was still raging, had been for days, and the lists of wounded and missing were not accurate as yet. So the days went by and Hilda came and went about her duties, with a great wistful look in her eyes and a heavy burden upon her heart. The boy's mother went feverishly about her many duties and worked all the harder, a smile upon her face that almost had the light of other worlds in it, so strong it seemed, and self-forgetful. Yet those who knew her best saw the strained look about her lips, the eager alertness in her eyes, the quick attention when anyone called or the phone rang or a telegram came. Some women would have taken refuge behind drawn curtains and wept. Not so Mrs. Stevens.

She was of old brave fighting stock. She knew her part and did it. The little gatherings for aid to the Belgians and French, for knitting and bandages and all sorts of succor, became only more frequent, and everywhere she was the moving spirit. She seemed anxious also to keep Hilda with her, and often when the girl really could not spare the time to be present at some one of these gatherings, she went because Mrs. Stevens almost insisted she should go.

Then, suddenly, like a bomb bursting at her feet, an incident, trifling in itself, occurred, which turned all her sweetness into sorrow and brought a cloud over her bright life.

18

Hilda had been pouring tea and passing little honey cakes made of corn and barley flour, and had not been noticing a newcomer who fluttered among them at a late hour and had not as yet been introduced to her. She was a girl about Hilda's own age, with exquisite features highly enhanced by the perfection of tinting and powdering, put on so imperceptibly that only the initiated were sure it was not real. There was something almost startling in the prettiness of her face, the delicate, high arched eyebrows, the long dark eyelashes, the faint shadows under the beautiful wide eyes, the rosebud mouth that could dimple or droop pathetically. Her dress was in the extreme of style, her frock cut a little lower at the neck, a little higher at the hem, a little scanter in the skirt than other girls wore, a daring little hat, perched giddily, that would have looked wicked but for the innocent, appealing rosebud mouth. Her little high French heels clicked when she walked, and her hands flashed with jewels. She was almost the first one of Mrs. Steven's friends who made Hilda feel utterly out of place. She glanced at Hilda with a careless stare, and a mere excuse of an inclination of her head backward when they were introduced, a stare that made Hilda feel herself considered a servant by the haughty beauty. She sported a priceless fur slung sideways on her shoulders with all the insolence of some queen of the forest, and she slouched into the latest curves of fashion with an almost dissolute ease.

"I'll take another lump of sugar in my tea!" she announced to Hilda peremptorily, and then turned to Mrs. Stevens who had just come up:

"Oh, Mother dear, when have you heard from Dannie! I'm just as worried as I can be! It's ages since I've had a letter. He hasn't answered the last one I wrote him."

Consternation filled the soul of Hilda. The tray trembled in her hand, and, regardless of the request for more sugar, she turned away and slipped softly into the shadow of a rich portiére. "Mother!" "Dannie!" Who was this unspeakable creature who claimed them both as if she owned them? A mad rush of jealousy seized her, threatening to fill her eyes with tears and her throat with sobs. Her heart seemed to be freezing in her bosom, and a sinking feeling came upon her. She knew only one thing, and that was that she must get away at once from them all like a hunted thing that has been wounded and wishes to hide its hurt. Setting the tray down quickly on a little table in the room beyond, she slid like a wraith through the library door into the hall and sped noiselessly up the stairs to where her wraps were left.

"Please tell Mrs. Stevens that it was getting so late I had to go. I did not want to interrupt her to say goodby," she said to the maid she met on the landing. Then she slipped away without being seen in the big room where they were all talking and clinking the teacups. The calendar said that it was almost springtime, but the weather as yet had given no sign. As Hilda came out into the dusky street a chill struck to her heart. She glanced back at the great house and felt as though she were saying good-bye to it. She seemed never to want to go there again. She wished she might go away from Philadelphia and forget it all. She felt ashamed and bereft all in one. For that girl had suddenly made her realize what she felt she ought to have known all along that she was not one of these people at all. She was an outsider, an intruder, brought there in a kind of sweet charity and allowed to think for a little while that all that beauty and richness and joyous life were hers as much as theirs; and now, here it was standing out in a clear light in all its ugliness! She was just a poor girl whom Mrs. Stevens had chosen to patronize for a while. This girl, this intimate beauty who dared to call her friend "Mother" had come, and with one look, one sweep of her jeweled hand, one uplift of her painted eyebrows, had shown her exactly how Mrs. Stevens's friends regarded her, as a mere protégé, with whom she exercised the sweet virtue of charity for the time being. And she, Hilda Lessing, had so far forgotten her portion in life as to bask in this precious friendliness, call it hers, and imagine it would last forever! Well, it was good that this girl of the world, the Stevens's world, had come this afternoon and cut away the mists, showing her the truth in all its ugly nakedness, so that she would be no longer under a delusion.

She excused herself from eating her supper on the plea of having eaten at Mrs. Stevens's, and then slipped away to her studies. But her mind was engrossed by deeper problems than any set by the university to prepare for the morrow, and when she finally closed her books in despair and lay down to toss for hours on the pretty white bed she was by no means ready for her classes. She thought that after a good night's sleep she would be able to concentrate her mind, and decided to get up early and finish her studying. But sleep would not come to her bruised spirit. When she closed her eyes she saw the haughty beauty, felt the withering of her slanted glance from half-shut eyes, and knew just how she, Hilda, appeared to the stranger as well as if she had carried a photograph she had just taken of her and turned it to her full view.

Even the little white bed and the silken curtain blowing in the moonlight reminded her of her position, warned her that she had been living in a sweet and dangerous dream.

And now, in the darkness, with the bar of silver moonlight across the deep blue of her rug, and the faint gleam of the silver things on her dressing table, she lay and faced the real trouble that she had heretofore kept in the back of her mind, and would not give way to. Daniel Stevens! That was the crux of the whole matter. The young man whom she had come to feel was hers — her friend, of course — but hers in the exclusive sense. His letters had grown to be the big hope of her life, his wishes, his approval, the measure on which she laid out her daily walk. And now here was this strange, painted, unpleasantly beautiful — yes, *beautiful,* for she would be honest — girl speaking as if he belonged to her; calling *her* Mrs. Stevens "Mother," and in every way appropriating, as if by old habit, the place that had come to be so dear to Hilda Lessing! It was horrible! It was unbearable! It was impossible! And yet by all that was dear and sacred she suddenly knew that it was not impossible, that it was quite the natural thing; and that she, the little school girl with the quiet, unfashionable past suddenly dropped down into society trying to be a fine lady was the impossible one. She had no business there and she must get out. It was all very lovely for these dear Stevens people to pick her up and help her to get an education, and be kind to her now and then by inviting her to a tea or a Red Cross meeting just to break the monotony of her hard work; but, of course, they had no notion of continuing this indefinitely. They knew she did not belong in their social set. They would not expect her to presume to stay there long. And she, how had she overstepped the bounds that her heart should have set? Her face burned red in the darkness, and she covered her eyes with her hands and groaned into her pillow. For the terrible truth had been forced upon her now, she was caring more than she had any right to care for the young soldier who had been so kind to her and written her such wonderful letters! And now, just when her heart was so filled with anxiety about him, and almost her every hour had been a prayer for his safety, had fallen this terrible blow upon her! She had no right to care this way! She was perhaps presuming even to pray in that possessive way! Her sensitive soul writhed in the torture of her self-accusing thoughts, even while her spirit sank aghast at the sacrifice that lay before her. He was not hers, he did not belong to her and never could! He probably belonged to this other girl who was of his world, and who would resent even a distant friendship with such as she; who would scorn and scourge her, and burn it in upon her that she had no right, just because she had done a simple duty and saved his life, to hang about his friendship for the rest of his life.

Ah! But that should never be! She would draw away within herself. She would show him when he came home — *if* he came home! A shivering sob went through her throat. She would show him that she had not taken his beautiful kindness for anything but a passing blessing. She would keep out of his world and walk her own way. It was going to be a little hard at first to gently and sweetly refuse the kindnesses his mother offered, but she must. Never again could she go and be one of that pleasant company. Her eyes had been opened. She had eaten of the fruit of the tree of knowledge, and it had had a bitter taste, but she would not overstep the bounds again. The girl might have her field to herself and welcome! She would never have occasion to cast that slanting, slithering glance again at Hilda's naked soul, for Hilda would take good care not to be about to receive it!

Some time toward morning she fell asleep and dreamed a troubled dream, but awoke with a start to hear her mother calling and to realize that she had only a half hour to dress, eat her breakfast and make her car for the university.

The morning was too filled with hard work to give her much time for thought, but she went about with a burden upon her heart and a cloud upon her spirits. Every time she lifted her mind to the experience of the night before a sharp pang warned her to keep back her thoughts.

She drew a sigh of relief as she came out of the last class and realized that there was nothing more for her to do for a little while and she might creep away home and try to rest her bruised spirit. Then as she came out upon the street she remembered that her mother had asked her to do some errands for her at Wanamaker's and she hailed a coming car, realizing that she was glad after all not to have to go back to the apartment yet where she would have to face all the pleasant things that Mrs. Stevens had done for her, as well as the big photograph of Daniel in his uniform that he had given her before he went to France. That, of course, she would have to put away now, where his handsome eyes could not watch her and smile to her as she sat at her desk studying or went about the room. How hard that was going to be! But she must do it, of course. She would make her heart understand that there must be no more dreaming. She had looked things in the face and she would not allow herself any toying with a fate that was not hers. Of course, it was not Dan's fault. He would have no idea how silly a girl could be about caring for him. He was not the least bit conceited, and he wouldn't think that she could dare presume to care the way she had. She dropped her eyes away from the crowding multitude in the car, and was glad they could not see into her heart and know what a fool she had been. "Oh, God!" she cried in her heart with her eyes closed and the car rattling along to the next corner. "Forgive me for being a blind little fool, and help me to be sensible and get over this so I won't trouble Mother!"

She bought the gloves and stockings and a few necessaries that her mother wanted, and stopped at the post office department to buy some stamps and a package of Government envelopes.

There were other things she ought to buy, but somehow she hadn't the heart today. She wanted to go home and lie down. She wanted to put that picture away and get it over with. It was going to be a hard wrench and she must get it out of sight before her mother came home. She put the envelopes and stamps in her coat pocket and turned away from the stamp window, going out toward the left to avoid the crowd, but as she lifted her eyes she caught the glance of familiar cold blue eyes. Her heart stopped dead still and then leaped on with a horrible bound. It was the air-man, just drawing his hand away from the post box where he had dropped a letter! Even while she looked aghast he dived behind a pillar and melted into the throng, leaving the swift impression behind him that he had both seen and recognized her!

19

It took but an instant for her scattered faculties to get to work again. All her heavy-heartedness was forgotten and she was on the alert. This was her job for the Government and for freedom. It had not been finished when she left Platt's Crossing. The enemies of the Government were still at large, and their absence was holding up a good many things that ought to be done. Here it was again; work, good hard work presented to her hand, and just when she was needing it to make her forget herself. Her spirit leaped to meet the need. Like an old trained spy, she slid behind the pillar and rose to her tiptoes. Was that his hat over by the silk bargain counter? Yes? No? She slipped around the marble pillar and up the white stone steps to the gallery, where she commanded a view of the seething aisles below, and leaning over she saw the flash of his eyes once more as they were lifted in a furtive glance that swept the gallery. But she, with senses keen, had the quickness to throw her gaze out over the multitude as if looking for someone else, and turn away, though all the time managing to keep him in view. She slipped behind a telephone booth and watched, and he went on down the aisle. She hurried past the telephone exchange and around to the other stairs, halting behind another phone booth just in time to see him pass the foot of the stairs going toward the Chestnut Street door. She kept herself out of sight until he had gone well on, then slipped quickly down the stairs and followed him, frantic now lest he should be lost in the crowd before she reached the street. It came to her that this was the great crisis of her life, the thing perhaps for which she had been born, to catch this spy and have him put where he could do no harm. She must follow at a distance and find out where he went, and then go and telephone the police, or Mr. Stevens or somebody. She could not think now, she must concentrate all her attention on keeping him in sight and finding out his hiding-place. Then she could slip back and notify the right people, and he would never know he had been followed, that is, if she did her work well. Of course, there was always the possibility that he might turn and see her again, and that would spoil it all, for if he thought he was being followed he would probably lead to a false trail. She must look out most carefully not to be seen.

He was shouldering his way through the shopping crowd, toward Thirteenth Street. He walked with a peculiar, gliding motion that carried him along very fast without seeming at all to be rapid. At times he slid between people in a way that reminded her of a serpent. Three times he disappeared for several minutes and she thought she had lost him, but just as he turned another corner he would square around and flash a glance back of him. Although he was so far away that his features were scarcely discernible, there was something so characteristic in his face as he turned it her way that she had an impression of cold, steely eyes piercing back half a block through the crowd after her. She wondered if he had really seen her in Wanamaker's and if he were uneasy about her following him. When she came to the corner where he had turned she stood close to the buildings and looked around cautiously until he had gone a long distance ahead. Then she sped along behind three ladies and kept herself well hidden for a time.

So she pursued him block after block, corner after corner, breathlessly, with no further thought for anything but her quarry. Her heart was beating so wildly that it seemed as if the people she passed on the street must hear it, and she noticed that some of them looked at her curiously. But on she sped, noting the names of the streets as well as she could, and keeping in mind the general direction in which she was going. It must be toward the river. Was he then going out at once to a boat that would perhaps take him to a submarine?

Hilda knew the general lay-out of the city well, for when they had first come she and Karl had spent much time over a great map of it hanging on the wall of the Stevens's library. Mr. Stevens had suggested that it would be a good thing for them both to memorize the names of the principal streets, so that they could easily find their way about. Hilda, always thorough in everything she did, accepted this advice literally, and quickly saw the use of it to them both. She kept Karl at it, working with him until they had mastered long lists of streets and made a sort of game of reciting them. So at night when they would all come home the mother and children would describe to one another the streets they had traveled that day, until at last it had come to be an old story, and the small map they had pinned up in their dining-room was only referred to when one or another of them went on some errand out of the usual beaten path.

So, as she hurried along, turning this way and that, she was able to keep a pretty definite idea of where she was going.

But the man she was pursuing was gaining on her. He had turned down toward the lower part of the city and was walking more and more rapidly now. He had ceased altogether to look behind him, although she had a strange, instinctive feeling that he knew she was there. She told herself again and again that she was foolish, that he could not know she was there, that he had shown no indication of any uneasiness. But still her impression lingered. He was more than a block away. If it had not been for his soldierly bearing and noticeable manner of walking she would not have been sure he was the same man she started out to follow.

As she strained her eyes ahead not to lose any new move he might make she was aware of a great weariness coming over her. The way ahead looked long and her heart seemed pumping painfully. If only there would be a policeman around to whom she might appeal! At this distance the air-man would hardly be able to recognize her and take alarm. But there was no policeman, and the people who passed were few and far between — nobody to whom she could turn for help. She had come a long way. Would the man never get to his destination and end this chase? She had half a thought of turning off to some side street and trying to telephone from a grocery store to Mr. Stevens, but just as she decided on this the man in the distance made an abrupt dash up some steps leading into one of the houses and disappeared from her view.

With all her nerves alert, once more Hilda quickened her pace, keeping her eye fixed carefully upon the house into which he had disappeared. At the corner she dashed across the street and walked more slowly down the block, trying to look like any lady out on business in the afternoon. The street seemed strangely empty. There was no one in sight in either direction. Did she fancy it, or was that a white face against the dark of the room, moving back from the window over there? That surely was the house into which he had gone. She hadn't taken her eyes from the steps for an instant. What was the number? 2217 — !

It was a dingy street of old red bricks built solidly, with little arched doorways between and with narrow brick tunnels to the back doors. Just in front of one of these Hilda paused and raised her eyes once more, as if casually to make sure and fix the number in her mind before going on down the block. The white face seemed to move across her vision back in the room again, 2217 burned in upon her brain, followed by a sharp breathless blank of utter darkness as a great hand reached out behind her and drew her into the passage and something dark and thick dropped about her face and enveloped her completely. She felt herself carried swiftly through a door into the passage, up stairs and stairs to the top of a house, and thrown heavily upon a hard bed. She tried to struggle, but it was all so sudden and her enveloping was so complete that she was helpless from the start. When her voice came back to her from some uncomprehending silences to which it had retreated in her first horror she tried to make sounds, but found them completely muffled and entirely inadequate.

Then she was still with fright. There were two men standing over her, and a woman's voice came puffing up the stairs.

"You petter stoff someding in her mouth. She vill yell und pring beeble! Here, take dis!"

The voice was unmistakable, and Hilda's

heart stood still with fright. Her enemies were upon her! She was in their hands! She was helpless and she would never be able to get word to Mr. Stevens where to find the air-man! What a fool she had been to go on past the house! How easy it would have been to run down a side street, call a policeman and make him watch the house! Oh, if she had only not been so careless and foolhardy! Here she had risked all, and now the knowledge she had gained was worthless, because the Schwarzes would make sure she would never get away alive to tell it. Perhaps they would even go so far as to kill her! It was possible that they might do worse than kill! Cold horror froze her into stillness. She lay like one dead.

"You sure you ain't kilt her?" Mrs. Schwarz's voice hissed cautiously above her now. "You dasent kill her, you know! The Captain, he vants her!"

"Oh, she ain't dead yet!" said a gruff voice that Hilda did not know, with a decidedly American accent. "She'll wish she was I bet before *he* gets through with her. She's only scared silly. She'll come round and yell like a loon. You better gag her now 'fore she gets a chance. When she comes to she'll make a lot of fuss. Where is the Cap, anyhow? He'll get us all in a mess if he sticks around."

Because a second sense told her to lie motionless with her eyes closed, Hilda forced herself to keep still as they threw the heavy blanket from her, disclosing her apparently unconscious form.

"He's ofer in his houze, across! He just telephoned. That's how ve knowed she was coming. He vill stay in the cellar till nide, und then he vill go to meed the submarine. He iss going to dake her mit him. There vill be nothing left pehind to make drubble, so you don't need to vorry."

"He hadn't ought to have stuck around this long! I told him so yesterday, but, of course, being captain, he know what he wants! Here! Give me that rag! Now you hold it so, in her mouth, while I tie it. Naw! That won't choke her. You don't suppose I want to kill the kid, do you? I never expected anything like this when I hitched up with this bunch! Now, give me that there string and I'll bind her hands behind her, and then we can lock her in and she can't do no harm!"

They forced an ill-smelling rag into her mouth and tied it around her head to hold it firmly. Then they rolled her over, bound her hands, and left her lying half on her face across the old straw mattress. The dusty breath of it smote upon her distress with a smothering sense and reminded her of the hour she lay in the old barn loft at Platt's Crossing. Strange! Here she was snatched as it were from the beautiful dream in which she had been living for several months and plunged back into the horror from which she had fled! Her work was all undone, and she was undone! There was nothing left for her but to pray to die! Her heart went up with a cry, "Oh, God! Oh, God!"

The choking of the gag was fearful, and the string around her wrists was cutting deep into her soft flesh. This was to go on for several hours, according to the plan Mrs. Schwarz had outlined. And the end was to be — a submarine! A submarine for her with the air-man as her master! Her heart almost stopped at the thought. She had read the tales of women whose awful fate had been to be prisoners on a submarine. She knew that death in comparison would be as nothing. The cold terror of it almost took her senses away. Then they came back with reeling revulsion as she heard footsteps again approaching and the key turning in the lock.

She knew by the hoarse apoplectic breathing that it was Mrs. Schwarz bending over her and listening. The woman lifted up one of her eyelids and looked at her keenly. Then she spoke in low, vindictive tones:

"Ach, you pad girl! You dried to ged us all in drubble, bud you didund make oud! You are in our hands now! You vill ged your medicine! My Sylvester and the cabdain they vill do vatefer they blease vith you. Your fine millionaire vrends vill hund for you bud they vill not pe able to find you. You vill pe under the sea! Do you hear that? You vill pe under the sea! Dake thad! Und thad!"

She hissed the words out into Hilda's stricken ears, and then struck her across her eyes and quivering cheek. The pain was keen, but the girl could only lie still and bear it. A great fear came over her that the tears would come and show the woman her triumph, and she prayed in her heart: "Oh, God! Don't let me cry!" It seemed a talisman that she kept saying over and over, till the woman closed the door and locked it, tramping off down the stairs with heavy tread, "Oh, God! Don't let me cry!"

20

When she was alone again the significance of all that had been said to her pierced to her heart and brain. Sylvester here, too! Sylvester and the Captain and all of them determined to take their revenge. Ah! Where were her friends, indeed! How could they reach her now! Only God could reach and help her. Surely God was stronger than the Schwarzes, stronger than all the Germans put together! Surely God meant to turn back these enemies of mankind and freedom some day and save His people. Surely! Surely! Wasn't she one of His? Could He, the great God in heaven, with all the universe to look after have time to care that she, little Hilda Lessing, lay in torment upon this old straw tick waiting for a swift unnameable awfulness to come to her?

"Oh, God, my Father in heaven," she cried with a breath of her soul, "come help me, please, now, and show me what to do if there is anything I can do. Forgive me for being such a fool and come and help me quickly from this terrible predicament!"

Then she rolled herself softly over and tried to stand up and look about her. Her head swam, and the gag and the cords about her wrists hurt horribly, but something must be done quickly while yet she was alone and had her senses. If there was no other way she must find means to kill herself. But first she must find a way to send word about the air-man. He must be caught, even if she died for it. But now was her time to do anything there was to do before anybody came back to watch her again. She must get those cords off her wrists and untie that gag. It could be done if she tried hard enough. God would help her. Her heart set itself to praying again as she struggled to her feet and looked about the room.

The shades were down at the two windows, showing long, slanting rays of light from the late afternoon sun where it crept through the scratches and pinholes in the old green shades. The room was papered with ugly dark paper and carpeted with a faded old ingrain, accentuating the darkness of the place. Besides the bed there was a bureau, washstand and chair. Several boxes, some open, some nailed shut, stood about the room and between the bed and the door was an old leather trunk with iron straps and rims. She would not have noticed it if it had not caught her dress as she started to move slowly toward the door. One of the iron rims was broken and bent upwards, showing a jagged edge. The girl gave a gasp of eagerness and slipped softly to her knees, backing up to the trunk and struggling to bring her wrists up to the broken place in the iron.

It was hard work, for her hands were tied in

such a position that she could scarcely move, and she could not, of course, see what she was doing behind her back. There was also the added problem of rubbing the cords back and forth over the rough iron hard enough to cut them without making any noise that might be heard below. She worked away for some time in a fever of horror and agony. The blood was running down her wrists, and the gag made her sick and dizzy. Once she staggered to her feet, the perspiration dripping from her brow, and crept softly, slowly about the room, trying to find some more effective means of severing her bonds, but finding none returned and went at the task more desperately, stopping every now and then to listen and make sure she had not roused her captors. But at last the cord gave way and she was able to loosen it enough to get one hand out.

Even then it was no easy task to untie the hard knot behind her head, and all the time her heart kept praying, praying, her fingers were cold and tense, with the thought of how the minutes were slipping away and she was doing nothing, nothing to save herself or capture the man who was making so much trouble for the Government! This thought would prick her lagging forces into action again, and she struggled with the knots until at last, with a final effort, she was free!

Her first thought on getting out of her fetters was to place a bar at her prison door that would keep her captors out. There was the trunk.

Dared she move it across the door? It was heavy as lead. But it would make a noise and bring someone up to see what was the matter, perhaps. However, she must try, and she must do it quickly. Every second's delay might be fatal. She got down beside the trunk, put her shoulder against the heavy box and was rewarded by feeling it move a little. She dared not move it more than an inch or two at a time. Slowly, painfully lifting one side and then the other, inch by inch it wheeled into place across the door, and Hilda sat down to breathe and think what next. At least she was safe for a few minutes. They could not easily push that trunk away before she had a chance to call out the window. But it wouldn't last for long. She must brace it somehow to the opposite wall. If she could only get a couple of those heavy boxes between one bed and the trunk the thing would be done. Softly she dropped to her task again, endowed with almost superhuman strength it seemed, and with a will that would not let mere weakness of the flesh prevail against her great need.

As the second box began to wheel into place her mind grew keen and she knew what she had to do. She must write a letter to Mr. Stevens. She had her fountain pen in her pocket and plenty of envelopes and stamps. She would put on stamps enough, write "Special Delivery" and drop the letter out of the window. She must not be seen at the window lest someone set to watch across the street might see her. That white face at the window! He would be on the lookout. He had a telephone over there. She must be very cautious. If she could get that letter out of the window when someone was passing perhaps it would be picked up and mailed. She must hurry! Oh, she must hurry for the time was going fast! The sun would be going down and it would be night and he would be gone, and — *she would be gone with him!* Then she thought of Daniel Stevens fighting over in France, and something rose in her to conquer. What were other girls and stations in life, and high or low, now? They were both fighting for their country! They were comrades! He would win out, and live or die as God pleased, and please God she would win out, too. She might die, she hoped she would, but she must win before she died. Before all else, that man must be caught!

She set her shoulder to the box and her will to the shoulder, and softly, with a velvet slide, the old box succumbed, slipped into the empty space, and the barricade was complete. With one breath of relief and assurance she got up and sat upon the box, feeling in her pocket for her pen and the little notebook she always carried. Then she wrote rapidly, the words tumbling upon the page faster than she could write them:

Dear Mr. Stevens:
I am shut up in the third story of a house some-

where down in the lower part of the city, near the river, I think. The Schwarzes are here. The air-man is across the street in a house numbered 2217. I followed him to see where he was staying and they caught me. He is going away tonight on a submarine —

The rapid pen paused just a second. Should she tell that he meant to take her with him? No, for it would kill her mother to know that. Better let her think anything than that!

The pen hurried on:

Send someone quick! I will draw a map of the way I went as nearly as I can remember after I left Wanamaker's. If anything happens to me and I don't come home tell my mother I was glad to die doing my duty. If I had been a boy I'd have gone to France to fight. I want her to be glad she had a girl to give. Please get here before dark or he will be gone! If I find any way I'll give you a signal where I am, but don't worry about me. Get the man first!

Hilda Lessing

She tore the sheet from her notebook and enclosed it in one of her envelopes, addressing it to Mr. Stevens's office, where he was usually to be found in the late afternoon. If he was not there his trusted secretary might open it or hurry it on to him. She wrote *Haste!* in large letters across

262

the corner, and "Important!" under that. She put on the usual postage and then ten cents in stamps and wrote "Special Delivery" as she had seen Mrs. Stevens do when she had no special stamp, and crept softly over to the window, taking care that she kept to the side of the shade where no one would see her from across the street. Cautiously she slipped her hand along the sash and turned the fastener, trying to push up the window, but it would not budge. She tried again, pulling the curtain down to hide herself, but the window was firm as a rock. She examined it carefully along the sides. It was nailed shut with two big nails driven through the sash into the window frame! She went over to the other window and found it was the same. Her heart sank and she slipped down on her knees and buried her face in her hands to smother a dry sob that came into her throat. She prayed again, "Oh, God! Help me! Help me to catch him before it is too late!" Then she lifted up her head and set her lips determinedly. She would have to break the glass! But how to do it so that it would make no noise?

She sat in thought a minute or two. If she should take something heavy, like her cloak, and lay it on the glass and then press hard against it, would that break it quietly? It would probably rattle down into the street and make a great clatter on the pavement, but she must take that chance. There was no other way. She must just trust that it would lie in the path and somebody coming along would pick it up and mail it. Was there a mail box in sight? She slipped to her feet again and peered out. Yes, she thought she had remembered it, just across the street. How wonderful! But, oh, would there be another collection in time? Well, the glass must be broken first and then if she heard the people below coming up she would fling out her letter before they had time to get in. Otherwise, she would keep it until she saw some one coming along towards the house.

Stealthily she collected what she needed for her purpose, a blanket from the bed, a slat that had evidently slipped out of place and lay beneath the bed. She looked up the street and down to see if it was empty. Then, with a prayer for help she arranged the blanket in thick folds where she meant to strike and drew back with the slat in her hand. First she leaned her weight with all her force against the slat and she heard the glass strain and crack, but still it remained. Drawing back a little she brought the stick forward sharply; there was a strain, a crack like the report of a toy pistol, and the glass gave way like a gasping thing, but not noisily, for the blanket deadened the sound, sending the fragments beyond the window sill. In a second more she heard them tinkling on the pavement below and she held herself still as death to see what would happen.

There was a minute of awful silence, during which she seemed to hear in her soul the tinkling echo of that glass striking on the pavement below. It seemed so little and insignificant compared to what she had expected, yet it seemed as if the whole universe could hear it.

A door slammed downstairs far away somewhere. The cry of a huckster in another street came acridly in with a whiff of cold air. A ragman's wagon rattled up the block and turned the corner, interrupting that awful silence. The door slammed again downstairs and the jagged glass in the window jarred noisily with the reverberation. Steps went heavily somewhere below and the window shivered again, but the steps did not come up as she had feared. It must be several minutes and nothing had happened yet! She drew a deep breath and pulled the window shade aside to peep out. All seemed still across the way. There was no sign or a face at the window now. There seemed no one in sight either up or down the street. A closer look revealed the fact that the two houses across on either side of 2217 seemed to be vacant. They had signs "To Let" in the windows. A sense of loneliness and desolation settled down upon her. She could not remember to have noticed the sound of footsteps going by since she had been in the room, although, of course, she had been too preoccupied to be sure. What if no one should pass in time? What if the post box were an abandoned one, because this region was so little peopled? But there! She must not think such things. She must trust in God. Surely He who had helped her get her hands free and move the boxes and break the glass silently would make the rest of the way smooth until she had done her duty. Her duty now was to catch that man and put him where he could do no more harm to her country, give no further help to the enemy of the world.

With a last look at her letter as if it were the only remaining link between herself and the world, she lifted her hand in a quick motion and flung it forth through the opening in the glass, stepping back at once so that she could not be seen if anyone watched across the way.

21

The letter, quite as if it understood, seemed to halt a second in the air and adjust itself to the breeze, then it calmly zigzagged itself down across in front of the next house and landed on the pavement face up with all its stamps glaring brightly, reassuringly up at her as she climbed a chair to watch through the crack at the edge of the curtain, as if to let her know it meant to do its best to get to its destination on time.

For fifteen long minutes she stood motionless on that chair and watched the letter lying there, her heart beating wildly at every sound in the house below. Oh, if the postman came before anybody had picked it up and put it in the box! She closed her eyes and prayed again, and slowly down the street came an old woman carrying a heavy market basket. Would she ever get opposite the house? And would she notice the letter and pick it up if she did? Hilda was so excited watching her as she came nearer that she did not notice the postman who suddenly appeared at the diagonal corner, produced his bunch of keys, opened the box, took out a single letter and slammed it shut again. The click of the lock brought her instant attention and her heart sank. She longed to cry out. Would he hear her? There was a noise below stairs. If anything called their attention to the letter now they might get possession of it and give her no chance to write another. Then while she debated wildly in her heart and the old woman paused and went up the steps of a house three doors away, the postman turned and came straight across the road, ran up the steps of the corner house, put some letters under the door, rang the bell and down again, stepping directly toward the letter. Her heart stood still with fear. He stooped and picked it up, gave one quick look at it, another questioning glance up at the row of houses and slipped it into his bag, going on down the street and across to the far corner where he left another bunch of mail and vanished beyond her sight.

She had not known how strained and stiff she was with anxiety until the strain was over. Now she slowly, painfully climbed down from the chair and sank on her knees beside it, hiding her eyes and letting a long, agonizing shudder go over her spent body. She was sore in every nerve and muscle. She longed to lie down now and die. Her work was done. She had tried her utmost. The letter would reach somewhere sometime, and there was nothing more for her to do, except to contrive a way to save herself if it were possible. But how could that be possible? She could break down the frame of the window perhaps and drop three stories to the pavement below, if she found herself unable to keep the enemy at bay, but that could hardly save her from them. It would be her last resort, of course, with a prayer that God would let it end her life quickly before they were able to put her to torture, but that, of course, must be her last resort. There was only a shadow of a chance that her letter might reach Mr. Stevens before dark, and someone might come to whom she could signal. She had seemed to know from the first that she was in an alien street, in a lonely region, where her cries would be practically useless, because they would reach the ears of her captors before they could bring any succor. It would be necessary to bring outsiders in some way if she were to be saved. The few who passed this way might not care to step aside and trouble themselves, and how easy the Schwarzes could say she was a crazy girl, confined there until they could take her to the asylum, even if she did succeed in attracting the attention of some stray passerby! Perhaps, toward evening, when people came home from their work to these houses, there might be enough of them together at once for her to take the chance to call out that she had been kidnapped and ask them to send for the police to rescue her; but certainly she would not risk it now with that awful Captain just across the street, watching perhaps, and no doubt in communication by telephone with all the powers of evil at the command of the German Government. Besides, who knew but Sylvester might come any minute? No, she would run no risks yet. But she must get up and discover the resources at her command. She must find out if there was any quick way of ending her life in case it came to that to protect herself against these fiends. Perhaps she might try tying the bedclothes together and letting herself down after dark. How would it do to get a sheet or blanket and wave it out that broken pane if anybody came by, and then call?

Stealthily she stole about her room, looking in the half-open bureau drawers, feeling in the open boxes. One contained thousands of pamphlets. She lifted one and saw it was something about peace. She wondered if this could be what they called German propaganda.

Another was an appeal to all loyal Americans to protest against the draft. But she had no time to look at such things now. She slipped a copy of each in her pocket and then smiled grimly at herself. She had no idea of ever getting out of this place alive, much less being able to communicate with her friends again. Why did she put these away? Well, perhaps if she dropped from the window they would find them about her and understand a little of where she had been imprisoned since her disappearance.

In the washstand drawer beside a half-used cake of brown soap, she found three matches! Ah! She clutched them and examined them closely to see if they were good. She could not tell, but if they were, here, indeed, was a means of signaling that would be more effective than anything else. The thought of it made her put her hands on her heart and draw a deep breath. Had she the courage to do it? Set fire to the room where she had barred herself from escape, except through the third story window? Well, why not? There were worse fates, and if the matches were good then surely God had sent them to her. She would have to wait awhile and see if her letter did any good. She would sit down and get quite calm and cool and think out what was best to be done. So, with her matches in her hand, she crept back to the window again and took up her station where she could pull the blind aside and watch the street. Three times as she kept her watch she was sure she saw that same white face flash up to the window, glance across the street and away again. Each time her heart contracted with a horrible fear and she heard again those sinister words spoken at Platt's Crossing, "She belongs to me! Understand?"

As the minutes dragged into an hour, and then two, and the sun's rays grew long and slant down the middle of the street from a golden west up beyond the city somewhere, her thoughts cleared. The time was nearing when she must act if act at all. And now she knew what she would do. It was five o'clock by the little watch that she wore. She knew Mr. Stevens would have left the office by now. If the letter had reached him at all, something would be coming soon. Also the darkness would be dropping down and then the air-man would be gone and she with him!

Softly she stole across the room and pulled the mattress from the bed, punching it carefully. Yes, it was straw. Straw would burn! But she ought to have more than that. She dragged it to the broken window and stood it up against the shade so that it leaned against the window frame. Then she gathered an armful of pamphlets from the box and began methodically twisting them as she had been taught to do in kindling a fire. All the time her heart was beating wildly, and she kept her glance out of the window as much as possible without actually getting in front of it. She heard footsteps coming rapidly down the street, and looking out again she saw a soldier coming hurriedly up the steps leading to the house in which she was confined.

Her heart leaped for joy for the instant and she forgot to guard against being seen from the window. Surely a soldier wearing the United States uniform would help her! She paused to think what she should do, and the front door slammed loudly and she heard the old familiar voice of Sylvester, calling loudly from the hallway below for his mother!

Her heart froze within her. Her body stiffened with fright. She stood still before the unbroken window with clasped hands and lifted eyes, praying aloud in her despair:

"Oh, God! Help me quick!"

Round the corner and down the street dashed an automobile and stopped suddenly in front of 2217. Four men got out and went up the steps. One stayed in the car. A face vanished from the dark of the room in the region of the front window and a message flashed over a wire — a wire that had been set in the dark of the night and never noticed among all the other wires the next day.

"That little devil in the third story has broken loose. She's standing at the window now. Better gag her quick and bind her well — curse her! They're after us! They're at the door now! I'm going to beat it, and you'd better get out while the getting is good, but mind you, bring the girl with you! I'll warrant you she's at the bottom of this, and we'll take our time and pay her well when we get to sea! Tell Mrs. Schwarz I'll hold her responsible for that girl. If she don't bring her I'll drown *her* in the middle of the ocean! So long! I'll meet you down by the river at the appointed time."

The telephone was in the cellar. The man hung up the receiver, pulled a soap box over it, opened a board door beside him and stepping through it drew it shut after him and fastened it. The four men above, grown tired of knocking, applied a pass key and stepped within the house.

Hilda, her hands still folded, her lips still murmuring a prayer, her eyes wide, stood watching in the window. There were noises below stairs. Hurried, heavy steps coming up, but she was not listening to them. She was watching, holding the three matches now in her trembling hand, waiting to make sure who these men were.

Slowly, stealthily the door of 2219 opened a crack and a face looked out. The man in the car was watching his comrades, one of whom was just within the doorway of 2217, but Hilda at the window saw the white of that haunting face and held her breath. The door swung open swiftly, a man came out, shut it carelessly and swung off the steps, walking briskly away with only a casual glance at the man in the car. It was *he!* He had somehow got into the house next door and was escaping! Nobody would notice him! He would get away again!

Regardless of what might happen to herself, regardless of her poor hands, she flung herself wildly against that window and beat frenziedly at the glass with her bare hands:

"Stop him! Stop him!" she shouted as if inspired. "That's the man you are after! He's a German spy! Get him quick!"

The man in the car gave a quick, comprehending glance upward even as he set himself in immediate action. Three sharp blasts on a whistle he gave and his car shot off down the street after the rapidly retreating Captain, who slithered around a corner and was out of sight.

The four men dashed instantly from the house and started in pursuit. Hilda could not be sure whether or not they heard what she said, but they looked up as they ran and seemed to listen. A second more and they were all gone, and she was aware of stamping feet coming up the stairs close by her door. Her time had come!

Dropping upon her knees beside the holocaust she had prepared she took the three matches in her trembling fingers and selecting the most propitious looking one, looked around for something to strike it upon. Suppose it did not light? Suppose she broke it before it lighted? Suppose all three were water-soaked with lying by the cake of soap! Sylvester was already at her door rattling with the key and shouting to his mother that he could not open it. "Oh, God!" she cried and drew the first match swiftly across the carpet.

22

Daniel Stevens had been gassed and taken prisoner after some daring feat of engineering in one of the big fights of the winter. By some gracious turn of events he had escaped after several months and returned to his company, but his superiors, after examining him carefully, and hearing his account of all he had suffered, sent him home on a furlough to recover his strength and grow fit.

The cable which he supposed he had sent his mother as soon as he was back in the lines, by the hand of one of his comrades, never reached her on account of some little mistake in the address. The comrade had written it down wrong. Stevens was sent to the hospital that night, and from there to a ship just starting, and so he had decided to surprise his people by dropping down upon them unexpectedly. He rested comfortably in the thought that of course they had received the cable that he was back in the lines again all safe. So long as they were not worrying he would just surprise them, and then his mother wouldn't have the anxiety of dreaming about possible submarines.

During the voyage he busied himself with a certain little leather book in which he had set down a record every day since he had been captured. They were the records of his inmost soul, and he meant to read them some day to someone

— but not yet. It was a good way to feel as though he were with those he loved, this writing down intimate thoughts that he might some time tell them. It kept him from dwelling upon some of the horrors through which he had passed, some of the things he wanted to forget. There were times when these things seemed to surge and roll over his soul like a consuming fire. At such times he had come to feel that there was only one thing that would save him from insanity and that was the thought of God over all guiding and controlling, and leading man up to some greater height where he might see his sin and know its remedy. For the first time in his life he saw the soul sickness of the world, and its great need of a God. He heard men on every side saying that there was no God, because He allowed such horrible things to happen; but he did not feel that way. And when he went among the boys who were going over the top he found among many of them a strong faith in the God who was to lead them over, and stay with them should it happen that they never came back. All the time he had been in the German prison camp he had had a feeling that God was with him, managing the whole thing, and he need not be worried. He realized that it was a strange state of mind for him to be in, for he had never taken much interest in religion, beyond attending his mother to church when she asked it. Now he had a real vital belief in God, not a mere theory that he had been taught and taken for granted without putting into practice, but something to live by and something to die by. There had been a night when he lay under the stars, weak and sick and unable even to crawl, with German guards a few feet away and live wires and machine guns on every side, and realized that he was in the hands of the enemy, with no one to help him. And then, whether awake or asleep, he knew not, he had a vision of One who came to him and spoke in the words he had reamed long ago when he was a child: "Fear thou not for I am with thee, be not dismayed for I am thy God. For I will strengthen thee; yea, I will help thee; yea, I will uphold thee by the right hand of my righteousness."

It came to him with a wonderful surprise, for what had he ever done to deserve this of God? If this had come from some ambassador of the United States Government now, he might have understood it, for he had been faithful and zealous for his country, and had not spared himself. But for God he had never cast a thought that was in any way serious or personal. His whole life thus far would have been lived no differently if there had been no God, so far as he could see looking back on it now. How strange that he had not realized before what a mistake he had made, what a lot he was missing, how ill-prepared he was to go out to meet death, knowing nothing of God nor how to die, save with physical bravery!

He knew that he must go home and somehow convey to his friends this message, this new gospel that he had learned out there on the battlefields. As he thought about it he felt shy of speaking of it to his mother and father. They had always shared each other's thoughts, yet they had never told him of this. They had spoken most intimately of the deeper things of life, yet there had never been a God in any of their talk. Only on the Sabbath when they went to church, had they recognized God, and that in a far-off, sort of patronizing way. Not that they meant to patronize, either; but perhaps they had never known Him and felt Him the way he had done in that German prison camp alone with God and his enemies.

There was just one person, when he thought about it, that it seemed as if he could talk with on this subject, and that was Hilda Lessing. She had seemed to take life so deeply and earnestly. She was herself seeking after the meaning of things. Her letters showed that; her beautiful, glowing letters, sweet revelations of herself. He had three of them that had accumulated at his post while he was a prisoner, and he carried them with him continually and read them often till he almost had them by heart. She had said she was praying that God would be with him and protect him, and somehow it seemed as if his vision must have been a sort of answer to her prayer. It seemed to him that he could tell her and she would understand. But he was afraid that his sweet, sane mother and his practical father might give him a troubled look and wonder if the gas had affected his mind just a little. He couldn't bear that now. It was too wonderful and sacred. He shrank from being misunderstood. Sometimes in his long meditations he half wished the folks at home could have a day or two at the front, just that their eyes might be opened and they might understand when the boys came home. It was hard to think that the ones you loved wouldn't understand — that they would expect you to go on and live the same as if the war had never been, and forget God. That was the sin that had brought the war on the world — forgetting God. The Germans had had to pay the heaviest price in the end because the Germans had started forgetting God. The great German universities had set the ball for forgetting rolling round the world, until everywhere the people had come to forget God. Now they must learn to come back and understand Him and be teachable. He would talk it all over with Hilda, and he would be deeply disappointed if Hilda didn't understand his feelings in the matter.

He was impatient over the landing in New York and the two-hour train ride home. It seemed longer than all the rest of the whole long trail. And when the train finally pulled into West Philadelphia and he hurried out, the thought thrilled through and through him,

"Home again! Home again!"

He took a taxi and lost no time in getting to his father's house. As he had hoped his father and mother were both there, his father having just come from the office, a weary, anxious look upon his face. There had been no word yet from all his inquiries at Washington about the boy in France. Strange that things should get so mixed up that their particular boy should seem to be utterly lost. If he was alive he surely would not leave them in this agony! The father was pacing up and down the library, and the mother looking out of the window, trying to keep a cheerful face above a heavy heart, when the door opened and the boy walked in upon them, with his old joyous ring in his voice: "Mother! Dad!" and was folded in their arms.

Half an hour later they were still sitting on the big leather couch, the son in the middle an arm around each. He hadn't even taken off his overcoat yet, and his trench cap was lying on the floor where he had dropped it when he stooped to take his mother in his arms. There was so much to tell, and so much to ask, and they hadn't really begun yet. When the servant tapped at the door with a letter that had just been sent over from the office marked "Haste!" and "Important!" the father frowned and was for throwing the letter aside. What could be of importance now that his son who had been dead was come home and was alive again.

It was the boy that caught sight of the writing on the envelope of many stamps, the same writing that had cheered his lonely sight in far away France many times, the writing whose every curve and line had become dear to him through long familiarity.

"Why, Dad! What's that? It's Hilda Lessing's writing. Open up and let's see what's the matter. Hilda never says important unless it is."

"Never?" said his mother playfully. "You speak as if you had known her always. Never is a long time, Son."

"Well, I have," said the boy half impatiently as his father tore open the envelope with an indulgent smile upon his face. But his father's expression grew serious as he read the letter.

"Why! Why!" he exclaimed, and, throwing down the letter he sprang to the telephone and called up the detective's office.

Dan caught up the letter as it fell and read, springing to his feet with a cry:

"Where's the car, Dad? At the garage? I'll have it at the door in two seconds! You'll come?"

The man nodded.

"But, Son!" said his mother. "You're not going away now, when you've just come and when you're — sick, you know —"

"I'm no baby, Mother! I've got to go! Hilda's been kidnapped! She needs me. I've got the letter, Dad!" and the erstwhile "invalided-home" dashed out of the room and away for the car.

23

Slowly, feebly the match burst into a flame, fizzled weakly and went out! Hilda caught her breath. Mrs. Schwarz was coming up the stairs now with the American behind her, swearing loudly. There was no time to be wasted. She took the second match and struck it sharply. The head broke off without a spark, and there was now only the meanest little old half match available. She nerved herself to do her best with it. She took the match carefully, held it close, struck with it firmly, and held her breath till it flickered up into a flame and blazed bright up the length of the stick. The moment was tense till it caught the first piece of paper, and then she drew her breath, and held another paper above the first and so on until the whole little pile was blazing and the edge of the tick began to scorch and curl and then blazed into a roar. It was started at last. In a moment more it would reach the window-frame and then it would be seen.

Somebody surely would pass, would see it and call the fire company! Would they get there before the door was broken in? She could hear the Schwarzes consulting outside in angry whispers. Schwarz himself was there. Sylvester, too, although they were hurrying him away. They had smelled the smoke and he, an American soldier in uniform, must not be found there if any-thing happened. He must get back at once to his barracks and know nothing about the affair. His father sent the other man down for a crowbar. They had decided to break in the door.

Hilda, kneeling beside her funeral pyre, was feeding it with pamphlets on peace, slowly, pain-fully, fearing lest her fire would go out before it had caught the woodwork and made blaze enough to be seen. She had promised to give a signal if she could. This was her signal. But the men had all gone after the air-man. There was no one left to see it and discover her plight. She must trust herself to God. Whatever He wanted for her was best, only not those Schwarzes. "Please, God, dear God, don't leave me to them!"

An angry blow came thundering upon the door, with curses in Schwarz's old familiar style.

Hilda stood up, her hand fluttering to her heart, and looked toward the door with wide, frightened eyes. The second blow split the upper panel in a long, slanting crack. She turned shud-dering toward her fire. Better fire than those fiends. And then, with sudden alarm, she real-ized for the first time what a thing she had done in starting this great power of fire in her defense. How the flames in that brief moment when her back was turned had licked their way up through the mattress and caught the shade and the window-frame and the paper on the wall.

The whole corner of the room seemed suddenly bathed in flame. Horrified, dazed with the heat, she retreated toward the other window, and, catching up the bed slat that lay on the floor, she dashed it through the glass of the other window, pane after pane, crashing through the framework with an almost superhuman strength. In a moment more she had a wide opening, and the cold air leaping in from outside sent the blaze roaring harder than ever. It helped to drown the noise at her door. With a sudden thought she caught at the water pitcher on the washstand. It was half full of water. She wet her handkerchief in it and then caught up a sheet that had dropped on the floor when she dragged away the mattress and soaked that. The upper panel of the door crashed in as she reached the window and climbed upon the sill. She turned frightened eyes and caught a glimpse of faces, wondering, angry, startled. Then a wave of smoke caught the draft from the hall and swept over them.

Shuddering, she turned her face toward the street and crept up on her knees on the window sill, with one dizzy glance down to the pavement. It looked as far as from earth to heaven.

Then, wild and clear there rose the cry of fire. A whistle screamed. Bells began to ring. They were coming! The blessed fire engines were coming! Oh, if she could make them hear, before the door gave way. It was very thick and wonderful, that wood. It did not break quickly with their blows. She could hear them tearing with their hands and trying to make a hole large enough for Schwarz to get through, for the American had declined to go. The smoke was troubling them. They could not see into the room for the fire was spreading toward the door. It had caught the corner of the wooden mantel, and one of the boxes was blazing. The carpet gave an ugly smudge that was stifling, and the smoke was pouring thick through the room. Up in the window where Hilda had climbed the flames were hottest of all. She reached for the sheet and wrapped it round her and put the wet handkerchief over her nose and mouth. As soon as they broke that door through she meant to swing out on the narrow window sill and be ready to drop if Schwarz laid a finger on her. Better the pavement below than his rescue!

The engines were clattering now; they were come, in flaring red paint and a gong, with a crowd following. She was alone no longer. They were all come, and were seeing her, and God and she stood up here together.

They were putting up a ladder now over the blazing, tottering way. They had seen her and were going to try to save her, but it was too late; the fire was almost upon her. She could feel its hot breath on her cheek. It had cast a wall of flames between her and Schwarz. Its kind, pro-tecting arms were reaching out and crisping up the floor between them, so that he could not walk to her. Kind, safe fire! It would all be over in a minute now. She could hear the voices in the hall hushed and fearful. "Quick! Over the back fence! Let me pass!" They went tumbling heavily down the stairs. Her soul laughed aloud in her triumph. The fire had conquered. Her signal had saved the day. What a pity the Schwarzes could not be caught, too. If only she could make the people hear above the din. Just one minute more to tell them! She thought of the soldier over in France. Perhaps he, too, was facing death. But she would not do her work half way. She must finish! She *must* tell them somehow before her captors got away!

She leaned far out over the window sill, pulling the handkerchief away from her face, swaying dizzily, and called in a clear voice that somehow made itself heard above the engines and the noise and the hissing of the water as it fell among the flames:

"They are getting away! The back fence! Quick!" she called, and "Go and catch them! They are all spies! The back fence! They have gone!"

Some of her words must have reached the people below for men dashed around to the alleyway. The flames and smoke were blinding her now. She did not see the car that came rushing up behind the fire engines, nor the young soldier who sprang past the guard in spite of detaining hands and dashed up the ladder toward her. She

had closed her eyes and pulled the wet handkerchief over her face again. She was sick with the
heat and the smoke. It wouldn't be long now, no,
it wouldn't be long! Was she falling? Or were
those arms that held her? Strong arms! God's
arms! Yes, that was it! "Underneath are the ever-
lasting arms!" She had known those words many
years, but, oh, it was good to feel what it meant
now. And this must be dying!

24

When she awoke she was in her own lovely blue and white room, with a wonderful smell of roses everywhere, roses that grew in the winter under glass and brought their perfume from the gardens of the great. She gazed at them, smiling at her everywhere. They seemed to have appeared so mysteriously in place of the smoke and flames, and among them on her dressing-table stood the picture, his picture, that she had been going to hurry home and put away before Mother should notice. Strange! Hadn't she been through all that awful experience at all? Had she only dreamed it after a wakeful night of fretting over that strange girl who seemed to be so intimate with the Stevenses? But no, her head and face were swathed in bandages and her hands were wrapped up, too. When she tried to move everything felt stiff and sore. This could not be heaven as she had at first supposed. People did not wear sore bodies in heaven. But it was good to be here. The quiet and safety, the perfume and the picture. Yes, the picture! She was too tired yet to contend with that picture. It smiled at her reassuringly. And, after all, it was hers. He had given it to her! So much of his friendship at least belonged to her! Why worry about it now? She closed her eyes wearily again and drifted away to sleep. When she awoke the next time it was all there, clearer and more defined, the picture was there and the roses.

Her mother opened the door gently and looked at her. "Are you awake at last, darling?"

There was something strange in her tone, as one speaks to one newly arisen from the dead, a kind of awe mingled with the love. Hilda tried to smile, but only her eyes accomplished it.

"Yes, Mother dear, I'm going to get up in a minute. Is it very late? I don't believe I'll go to the university today, I feel a little tired." Her voice trailed off weakly.

"No, dear, you won't go to the university for a day or two, at least. You're going to lie still and rest for ever so long till you feel like getting up."

"But I must get up!" she stirred uneasily. "There's something I must find out —"

"No, dear! You needn't worry about anything. Mr. Stevens will tell you all you want to know when he comes back. He's very anxious to see you as soon as you are able. You were very brave, and everything is all right. Now go to sleep, and when you wake up again I will phone him. He has gone to lie down. He isn't very strong himself, and carrying you down the ladder was a heavy strain."

"Did he bring me down?" she asked wonderingly. "I didn't know I came down. I thought I was going to stay up there."

"There, dear! Go to sleep!" Her mother drew the shade down a little lower and slipped away, closing the door. Hilda opened her eyes again and saw the picture smiling at her, and drifted off to sleep with the thought in her mind that she must ask her mother to put away that picture before Mr. Stevens came. He would think it presumptuous in her to have his son's picture in her room. But why had her mother said that he wasn't very strong yet himself? Had he been sick? She hadn't heard about it.

When she woke again, the picture had come alive and was sitting in the blue velvet chair by her bed with one of its hands in a bandage. She looked at him in bewilderment, and then back to the picture on the dressing-table, and wondered if she were still in the strange, dazed land between two worlds where everything was queer. Then he spoke softly in a joyous, hungry voice:

"Aren't you ever going to wake up and speak to me — dear?"

The last word was breathed rather than spoken. When she thought of it afterwards she wasn't sure that she had heard it at all.

"Is it really you?" she asked bewildered, "or am I dreaming? I thought you were in France!"

"It is really me!" he said smiling. "Didn't you know me last night, dear?"

"Last night! Was it you? But I thought Mother said it was your father. Then *you* carried me down the ladder! Oh! And you are wounded! Your hand is all bandaged!"

"Not wounded. Only a trifle scorched. You

gave me a pretty warm welcome, you know."

"*You* saved me, and got *burned!*" she breathed tremblingly. "Oh, how can I ever repay you?"

"By marrying me just as soon as you are able," he said, smiling audaciously. "I'm just about sick of this half-way business. I want the right to take care of you. If I have to go back to France again soon I want to fix things so you can't get kidnapped again, or go around doing Secret Service work for the country any more. I want you to understand that you have served your term. You shall receive a Croix de Guerre or its equivalent and be honorably discharged from the service. You certainly have done your bit several times over, and I'm not going to run any more risks with you. You are far too precious to me. Why that trip I took from our house down in the car to find you was ages long. It almost turned my hair gray. I knew then that if I found you I'd keep you safe where no Schwarz or German spy could come near you again."

"Oh!" said Hilda in a sweet little scared voice from out her bandages. "Did they catch the air-man and Schwarz?"

"Caught the whole bunch of them! Rounded up the air-man down by the river just taking to a boat he had hid in the bushes. I believe they caught the Schwarzes trying to climb the back fence. They've got the gang shut up safe and sure, waiting for you to get well enough to identify them before they go into seclusion out at some fort or other in the west, where they will be forcibly prevented from doing any more harm this session. Now, I'd like an answer to my question. I told you that I loved you. Will you marry me?"

For answer Hilda raised her eyes and gave him one long, troubled look.

"Who is Gertrude Gilchrist?" she asked irrelevantly.

"She's a little silly-headed fool that is always trailing around trying to take on notice. She's dogged my steps ever since I got my commission. She's uniform-crazy. What on earth has she got to do with the subject? Has she been nosing in on this combination? She's a nut! She's a mess! What have we got to do with her?"

"She called Mrs. Stevens 'Mother,'" said Hilda in a troubled voice, "and she spoke as if she corresponded with you."

"She did, did she?" said the young man, noting with satisfaction the changing color on as much of Hilda's face as was visible. "Well, she does; she writes me loads of invitations which I never answer, and sends me postcards with her picture in fancy costumes that she has worn at a play for some war benefit, and I put them in the waste basket! Do you know what Mother and I call her? The vampire — 'vamp' for short. Oh, you peach blossom! Oh, you darling! Did you *care?* It's the first good turn she ever did me in her life, if you care! And now, answer my question —

Will you marry me right away?"

The bandaged head shook a decided negative:

"Not till I've had an education."

"Education be hanged! Haven't I got education enough for us both? Did you think I wanted to marry a schoolmarm? No, of course, I didn't mean that. You shall study as much as you want to — *after* we are married. We'll study together! Why wait for an education?"

"Because I'm not in the least fit to be your wife now. I've got to be somewhere near your equal, in knowledge, at least, before I could think of it. I'll see what I turn out to be. I'm not going to have your friends despising me and pitying you!"

Daniel Stevens threw his head back and laughed.

"Are you judging my friends by that little feather-brained idiot? I'll warrant you had more real knowledge when you were five years old than Trudie will ever have. The only school she ever finished was dancing school, and she couldn't jump on a train when it was going nor light any kind of a fire even in a fireplace if her life depended on it. She's a poor little fool! Talk about being my equal! There's only one thing I'm not dead certain you're not my superior in, and that's in loving me as I love you. Of course, there's no comparison between the two things, for look how wonderful you are, and what am I that you should love me? But say — do you think you *could* — just a little to begin on?"

He was bending anxiously over her now, his eloquent eyes pleading, his voice rich and tender with emotion.

"Could you — darling?"

With a swift beautiful motion of claiming their own, Hilda's bandaged hands went round his neck and drew his face down close to her lips. But what she whispered only those two heard.

We hope you have enjoyed this Large Print book. Other G.K. Hall & Co. or Chivers Press Large Print books are available at your library or directly from the publishers.

For more information about current and up-coming titles, please call or write, without obligation, to:

G.K. Hall & Co.
P.O. Box 159
Thorndike, Maine 04986 USA
Tel. (800) 257-5157

OR

Chivers Press Limited
Windsor Bridge Road
Bath BA2 3AX
England
Tel. (0225) 335336

All our Large Print titles are designed for easy reading, and all our books are made to last.